THE LOVING HEART

Lily Ross becomes nursemaid to young Mary, whose widowed father runs Frobisher's Emporium in their seaside village in Devon. She loves her job caring for Mary, a good-natured and spirited child. Although Matt, her fisherman friend, worries her with his insistent love that she cannot return, other things fill her life: Mary and her adventures, the strange flower lady — and her growing feelings for her employer, Mr Daniel. But as his nursemaid she must keep her feelings to herself, or risk losing her position . . .

CHRISTINA GREEN

THE LOVING HEART

Complete and Unabridged

LINFORD
Leicester

First published in Great Britain in 2014

First Linford Edition
published 2015

A catalogue record for this book is available
from the British Library.

ISBN 978–1–4448–2548–0

Published by
F. A. Thorpe (Publishing)
Anstey, Leicestershire

Set by Words & Graphics Ltd.
Anstey, Leicestershire
Printed and bound in Great Britain by
T. J. International Ltd., Padstow, Cornwall

This book is printed on acid-free paper

1

I was delivering loaves to the café when Jess said, 'Come over here, Lily. There's something I want to tell you — something important.'

Her saucy eyes were bright so I followed her into the back of the shop, and she turned and said, 'I've just heard that Mr Frobisher's nursemaid has had to leave because of her mother's illness, so Mr Daniel wants someone else to look after his little daughter Mary. Now's your chance, Lily. Always saying you wanted a better job, aren't you?'

I know my eyes opened a bit wider. A situation in the Frobishers' house on the seafront? That lovely house where, from all I'd heard, the furniture gleamed with polish and silver, and pictures decorated the rooms, and old Mrs Frobisher was dressed in silks and satins. Of course I would love to work there! It would certainly be much better than slaving away in Aunt Edie's bakery, where she gave me all the hard jobs and very little praise.

I smiled. 'Thank you for telling me, Jess. I'll go straight round and apply.'

I left the café and ran down the Esplanade, heading for the row of big, tall houses where the Frobishers lived. At Number Three I went in at the tradesman's entrance and knocked at the door, which was opened by a woman with a smudge of flour on her red face.

'And what do you want?' she asked briskly.

I took a big breath and said, 'My name's Lily Ross, and I'd like to apply for the situation of nursemaid to Mr Frobisher's little girl, Mary.'

'So it's got around already, has it? What gossip!' she said with a sniff. 'And that means I shall have girls thumping on my kitchen door all day long. Well, Mr Daniel's not here — he's at the shop — so you'd better go round there and ask to see him.' And she shut the door in my face.

I went through the town and into Frobisher's Emporium, where the woman at the cash desk said, 'Asking for a situation, are you? Well, go over there and sit down and I'll ask Mr Daniel if he can spare a minute to see you.'

I waited in a little room just off the dress-material department and thought about the shop. It was our town's favourite centre, and I knew that Mr Daniel had inherited it from his father, old Mr Edward Frobisher, who had first started it after having a stall in the nearby market town for several years.

While I waited, I went on a little memory trip about the shop. Bed linen, haberdashery, ladies' hats beyond the menswear upstairs, and a large ladies' dress department down here at the back of the shop. In fact, a place where you could be sure to find whatever you wanted.

I felt sorry for Mr Daniel, who I

thought was a nice, polite man who usually had a smile for his customers. Since his wife had died a few years ago, though, he had become leaner and more serious-looking. And now, as his little girl's nurse had had to leave, he must be worried about who was going to look after her. I knew old Mrs Frobisher, his mother, was fond of the child, and probably did her best with the servants' help; but of course a real nursemaid was needed. From what I'd heard, young Mary was quite a handful. But I had a feeling I could fill that position easily and with pleasure. I liked children and often took Jess's young brother, Bobby, out for a walk when I had an hour off.

I was thinking all this when the door opened and Mr Daniel came in. I got to my feet and looked at him: tall, thin, dark-haired with a neat beard, and eyes that looked dull and sad. At once, sympathy rushed through me and I smiled at him.

He looked at me very carefully, then

said, 'I understand you are applying for a position, Miss . . . Miss . . . er?'

'Ross,' I said at once. 'Lily Ross. Yes, sir, I heard that your nanny has had to leave and so I wondered — I thought that perhaps . . . ' Words failed me, but I took hold of myself and managed to complete the sentence. 'You see, I would love to look after your little girl for you, Mr Daniel. I mean, someone's got to do it, haven't they? And if you'll have me I can get a reference, I'm sure. I'm clean and capable, and . . . ' Again I halted.

He looked at me with those intense, dark eyes, and slowly a hint of a smile lifted his lips. 'And you're a kind girl, Miss Ross. I can see that.' He paused, then asked, 'Well, where do you work at the moment?'

'At my aunt's bakery — Radford's, in Regent Row. But I'm only filling time there. You see, I really want something better than having to push dough around all day and sweep up all the spilt flour.'

I thought his straight mouth lifted just a little and he said, 'Radford's. Yes, I know it. But won't your aunt miss you, Miss Ross, should I give you a situation here?'

Instantly I thought of Aunt Edie and the way she gave me all the clearing-up jobs to do. 'No,' I said very definitely. 'There'll be lots of young girls wanting to fill my place. I shan't be missed.' I knew that because she was always hinting that I ought to be somewhere else doing something else. Indeed, I thought she wanted to get rid of me. So I gave Mr Daniel an even bigger smile and was pleased to see him smile back.

He cleared his throat, stroked his beard, and then said, 'I do believe you might suit my family, Miss Ross. Would you be prepared to give the situation a trial, say for a few weeks, before we make a permanent decision?'

'Thank you, sir,' I said quickly. 'I would certainly be ready to do that.'

I wondered what my wage would be, but he must have read my

thoughts as he named a sum that was in excess of what I had imagined, and added: 'You will have a bedroom of your own next door to the nursery, and I know my mother, Mrs Frobisher, will welcome you. At the moment she is looking after the children with the help of the servants, so could you start very soon?'

'Yes,' I said certainly. 'I could come now, if you would like me to.'

He smiled again then, a warmer smile, and I returned it.

'Shall we say this evening, after the shop shuts? About seven-thirty?'

'Thank you, Mr Daniel,' I said. 'Yes, I'll be there. And thank you again. Goodbye.'

I turned and left the emporium, walking with wings on my heels, back to the café where Jess turned briefly from her waiting at table, and grinned when I told her the news.

'There! Told you to be quick off the mark, didn't I? Working for the Frobishers! And I suppose you'll wear a

smart uniform, won't you, white cap and dark dress and huge white apron!' Then her smile faded. 'And what does your Aunt Edie think about this? Have you told her yet?'

My own smile disappeared. 'No,' I said. 'I'm going back there now, to tell her.'

Jess nodded at me. 'Good luck,' she said, then turned to welcome a new customer.

★   ★   ★

Aunt Edie was sitting quietly in her little room off the bakery kitchen. She held a mug of tea and had her feet up on a stool. She looked at me with hard eyes when I entered.

'And where've you been, miss? Just when I needed you, you'd gone. Well, the sweeping-up's waiting, so get on with it, if you please.'

I set my lips and stared at her. 'I've got another situation, Aunt Edie,' I said quietly. 'I shall be starting it this

evening. But yes, I'll do the clearing-up before I go.'

She swung her feet off the stool and stood up, spilling a drop of tea as she did so. I thought she looked upset, so I added, 'I'm sorry, but I'm sure you'll get another helper very quickly. And I always said I wanted a better job, didn't I?'

Her face had gone quite pale, and I watched her reach out to put a hand on the nearby table. 'Oh yes,' she said, 'after all the years when I took you in and looked after you, now you're off, and just saying sorry.'

I frowned. 'Well, what more can I say? And of course I'm grateful to you for taking me in when Ma left . . . '

'When she *left?*' Aunt Edie was screeching now. 'You mean ran off!'

The room seemed to get very hot and I felt my heart thumping. 'Ran off?' I echoed. 'But you always said . . . '

She finished the sentence. 'Of course I didn't tell you the truth — you were only a baby when she went. But now

maybe it's time you knew. Your ma ran off with a gardening man from Exeter and I've never heard a word from her from that day to this.'

We stood in the middle of the room and stared at each other and I felt suddenly very sorry for poor Aunt Edie, who had kept this secret while she was bringing me up for so many years. And now I was leaving her. What must she be feeling? And could I really go? Shouldn't I go back to Mr Daniel and tell him that I had changed my mind?

My thoughts ran in circles, but at last I said very slowly, 'I'm grateful, Aunt Edie, for everything you did for me. But it's time for me to find my own way now, and this is such a chance. I'll keep coming to see you, of course, but I have to go.'

I left the room, went upstairs to my little bedroom in the attic and started packing my few belongings. I was terribly sorry for Aunt Edie and hoped that perhaps in the future I could make better friends with her and in some way

repay her for all her care of me as a child.

And as I packed up I thought of my wicked ma who had run off with a gardening man. How could she have left her baby daughter? I wondered. Leaving a child alone! And that made me even more determined to prove myself with Mr Daniel, and show him how well I would care for little Mary.

* * *

I presented myself at the back door of Number Three the Esplanade at one minute to seven-thirty, and this time a housemaid in a dark dress and white apron opened it. She smiled at me. 'Are you Miss Ross?' I nodded, and she opened the door wider. 'Please come in. Mr Daniel and Mrs Frobisher are waiting for you in the drawing room. Follow me.'

The drawing room? I tightened my grip on my shabby old valise and took a deep breath. Was I looking tidy enough

11

to be a nursemaid? I had sponged my coat and brushed my hat and polished my boots, but I knew I didn't fit into this lovely room, where two figures waited for me.

'Miss Ross,' said the housemaid, and disappeared. I stood there and wondered whether I should speak first, but already Mr Daniel was coming towards me, holding out his hand and smiling. I dropped the valise and took his hand. It was strong and warm and I thought I felt a sort of welcome radiate through it. And my nervousness died away as he said, 'You've come in good time, Miss Ross. This is my mother, Mrs Frobisher. Mother, this is Lily Ross, who is coming for a few weeks to see how she and Mary get on.'

The tall woman with grey hair and a very straight back stood there, looking at me. But she smiled a bit and nodded. 'I welcome you, Miss Ross. My son tells me you are fond of children and are looking for a responsible situation such

as this. What experience do you have?'

I swallowed the lump in my throat. This was the all-important moment. I couldn't lie, but somehow I must make the overpowering Mrs Frobisher understand that I would be a good nursemaid.

'I haven't worked with children before, but I sometimes take friends' children out for walks, and for visits to the museum, and sometimes to do their shopping.' I stopped. Then I added in a faint voice, 'And I believe these children have grown fond of me . . . '

Mrs Frobisher kept looking at me with those piercing eyes, but she said, after a second's pause, 'Well, let us see what Mary thinks of you, shall we? Daniel, ring the bell, please.'

He went to the wall beside the fire and pulled a rope. After a minute or two the door opened and a small girl was ushered in by the housemaid. She ran to Daniel without looking at me.

'Papa, I was waiting for you to come up and tell me a story. But Nancy said

you want me down here, with Grand-mother.' Then she looked around her, and I saw her bright blue shining eyes focus on me. I felt something warm and pleasant pass between us, and then, with a shy smile, little Mary came up to me and said, 'Hallo. Who are you?'

'I'm Lily,' I answered, and went down on one knee to look into her pretty face. 'And would you allow me to tell you your bedtime story this evening? I'm good with stories. I know one about a little girl like you, with blue eyes and a big smile, who lives in one of the boats in the harbour. Would you like to hear it?'

Mary turned to look first at her father and then at her grandmother, and when they both smiled and nodded, she put a hand on my arm and said, 'Yes, please. We'll go up to my bedroom, shall we, Lily?'

I knew then that for some reason, Mary and I would be able to get on together.

2

Mary's nursery was a big, spacious room with fairy-story figures painted on the walls and an old rocking horse which I at once imagined Mr Daniel riding as a child. A small fire crackled in the hearth, and two big windows with floral curtains gave views of the sea and the river flowing out beyond the Point.

Mary led me into the connecting small bedroom where her nightdress and robe were spread out on the bed. 'I'll get undressed,' she said. 'I can do it myself. Nanny, who had to go and look after her mother, said I was a very ca . . . ca-pable child.' She looked at me and smiled mischievously. 'Have I got the word right, Lily?'

'Yes, you have,' I said, smiling back. 'I think I shall learn many more big words from you, Mary. Now, can I help you

brush your hair?'

She sat on the edge of her bed with me beside her, and as I brushed the fine, pale hair I started the story of Becky who lived on a ship in the harbour and had exciting adventures. We were well into the final moments of the story, with the adventure coming to an end, when the door opened and Mr Daniel came in.

'Papa!' Mary flew to his side and he bent and kissed her. 'Lily knows some good stories,' she told him, and he looked at me and smiled.

'I won't stay and interrupt,' he said, walking around to the other side of the bed, taking her with him. 'I just want to say goodnight to Mary, and then I'll leave you to finish the story.'

He bent down and put his arms around her. I sat there, feeling awkward at watching this intimate moment in their shared lives. But Mary was kissing him and cuddling into his arms, and giggling at something he quietly whispered in her ear, and then it was over.

He stood up, smiling down at her. 'Into bed then, and sleep tight. And I'm sure Lily will think of something exciting to do tomorrow.' He walked to the door, then turned and looked at me. 'Of course, you will have your meals with us in the dining room, Lily — but have you eaten tonight?'

I shook my head. Food had been the last thing on my mind when I left Aunt Edie's.

'Then Nancy will bring you up a tray for this evening. And let me show you your bedroom — in here.' He led me towards a small room next to the nursery and stood in the doorway while I looked around me with a gasp of pleasure. So different from my squalid little room in the attic back at Regent Row — not big, but warm and airy, with pretty curtains over the one big window, a bed covered with a colourful patchwork quilt, a dressing table with a mirror that had no foxing on it, and a small wash basin. It was heaven after what I had been used to.

My voice was uneven as I said, 'It's lovely, thank you, Mr Daniel. I know I shall sleep well in here.'

Our eyes met and we smiled at each other. Then his face straightened and he said in a very low voice, 'I'm sure you will do all you can for my daughter, Lily. Mary missed her mother badly when she died, and now that Nanny Brooks has gone, that is another warm person missing from her life. You see, she needs loving.'

I nodded, while one big thought spread through my mind. '*And so do you, Mr Danie . . .* ' but I said nothing, just turned aside and wondered who, in his busy life, might be the one person to give him what he so badly needed. Of course he must have lots of friends; and surely a few of the customers in the shop, who knew him well and probably invited him to dinner, would have ideas about marrying him — a well-to-do shopkeeper who was handsome, of marriageable age, and with a kind and

understanding attitude to the world about him.

He stepped away then and said we would meet in the morning at breakfast, and I heard him call goodnight again to Mary before he went downstairs. I went back into her bedroom, where she was snuggled in her bed, and somehow managed to finish the story of Becky in the ship having the adventures.

But when I finally got into my own bed, my few belongings packed away and the gas turned off, I lay there listening to the gentle lapping of the sea on the beach just beyond the house, and wondered when I should meet the man of my dreams. And why should I spend so much thought on Mr Daniel when my own life was empty and loveless? I turned over, telling myself that with this new life opening up for me, I would most certainly soon meet someone I could love. And then I slept.

★   ★   ★

In the morning I helped Mary dress, then took her downstairs into the dining room where Mr Daniel and Mrs Frobisher were waiting for us. I was greeted with smiles and a hope that I had slept well, and slowly I began to settle down in this elegant and beautifully furnished house.

Mrs Frobisher, dressed in a plain but smart dress with big sleeves and a high collar, asked me what I had planned for the usual morning outing.

'Mary is always taken out for a walk before luncheon,' she said. 'Perhaps along the Esplanade, or possibly around the Point to the river beach, to watch the ferry as it comes across from Shaldon. She likes to see the boats, and the fishermen mending their nets.'

'Yes, Mrs Frobisher, that sounds a very good idea. We'll take a turn along the front to see the donkeys, and then go round to the river beach. She'll have a good appetite for luncheon then.'

Mr Daniel kissed Mary before leaving for the shop, and gave me a

smile over his shoulder as he went. Mary and I went upstairs to the nursery and did a little reading and then some drawing, and the morning passed happily. Then we put on our coats and hats and went out onto the Esplanade.

Out of the house Mary became even more spirited and energetic. She had me running after her, one hand on my hat and other reaching out for hers, which was always just out of reach. When we got to the river beach she halted and looked at me breathlessly, her eyes sparkling with pleasure. 'I can run faster than you, Lily! And now I want to see the boat where Becky lives.'

That was a problem, but I soon found the answer. 'Becky has gone out with the trawler men today, fishing for mackerel. She'll be back again later in the afternoon, with another adventure for you to share at bedtime. Now, I have an idea — why don't we walk back to the little café where my friend Jess works? I know she'd love to meet you, and we might even have a drink of

lemonade there.'

Mary nodded, and so we left the river and walked sedately back along Powderham Road and into the Seaspray Café, where Jess was busily setting out cups and saucers on the tables which filled the little room. 'Well,' she said, smiling, 'looks like you got the situation, Lily — and who is this pretty little girl, I wonder? Could it be Miss Mary Frobisher?'

We sat down at a table and Mary smiled up at Jess as she asked, 'May I have some lemonade, please? And how did you know my name?'

Jess looked down into the curious face as she said softly, 'Because everybody loves you, Mary, and you're quite famous.'

'Famous!' Mary was pleased and fidgeted in her seat. 'Thank you, Jess — and, oh where did these lovely flowers come from?' She stared at the small bowl of primroses decorating the table and touched them with her fingers.

Jess moved away to find glasses and a big jug of lemonade, then came back, saying, 'We bought them from the lady who sells flowers every day. She comes into the town with a big basket and goes from shop to shop. Last week she brought violets, and now it's primroses.' She paused, looked out of the window, and then nodded her head. 'Look, there she is — and she's only got a few bunches left in her basket. I expect she's on her way home.'

But Mary was on her feet before I could stop her, darting to the door, opening it and calling out, 'Please don't go away! Your flowers are lovely and I want to give a bunch to my grandmother. Can I have one, please?'

I got up, following Mary outside. The woman, her lined face slowly lifting into a smile, looked at me and said, 'Does the little miss really want a bunch? Well, I've only got a few left and she can have them all, if you like.'

I was at a loss as I carried no purse, not realizing that Mary might want to

buy something. I said, 'That would be very nice, and thank you, but I have no money on me.'

The woman picked up the remaining bunches and tied them together with a thread of wool. 'I'll be here tomorrow,' she said. 'You can pay me then. I'm always doing the streets first thing in the morning, selling the flowers when they're fresh, you see.'

Something about her intrigued me. She was middle-aged and her dark hair showed a few grey hairs beneath the bright scarf tied around her head. Without really thinking, I asked, 'Where do you live? Do you come far? And I suppose you walk into town?'

She looked at me curiously. 'I do. I live just outside town, in Rose Cottage, and I grow all the flowers in my garden. If you're interested you can come and see it. Bring the little maid; she likes flowers, doesn't she?'

I was surprised, but Mary pulled at my arm and whispered, 'Oh, I should love to go and see the flowers growing.

Can we go another day?'

'Perhaps,' I said, wondering if Mrs Frobisher would be shocked at the idea, but hoping we could go. 'We'll be here tomorrow morning,' I said to the woman. 'I'll pay you then, and yes, we might come and visit one afternoon. I expect Mr Frobisher would let his groom drive us to your home.'

'So you work for Mr Frobisher? The one who runs the emporium? I remember him.' The woman smiled suddenly, her face lifting into a happier expression. 'What's your name, miss?' she asked.

'Lily,' I replied, without thinking about it.

'Lily.'

I watched her; suddenly she looked not so old, not so bent and poor. She must have been a pretty young woman, I thought; but then she was back into her lined, impersonal expression, holding out the big bunch of primroses and saying 'Goodbye' quietly, and walking away up the road, her basket empty.

She soon disappeared around the corner.

But not out of my mind. I went back into the café and as Mary and I finished our lemonade I said to Jess, 'Who is that woman? She seems — strange . . . '

Jess cleared a table beside us and said, 'Yes, a bit odd. She looks lonely, I think.' She looked at me curiously. 'Will you go to see her? Fancy her inviting you . . . as if she wanted to see you again.'

I helped Mary to her feet and we headed towards the door, Mary clutching her precious flowers as she went. 'I don't know, Jess,' I said over my shoulder. 'But of course, I shall have to ask Mrs Frobisher for her permission to go.'

'I hear that she's very stern. But let's hope she'll let you take the child out and amuse her. It's probably what she needs.'

I didn't answer, but knew I should try and persuade Mrs Frobisher to allow us to do all sorts of interesting

things. Mary was an intelligent little girl and needed entertaining. I smiled at Jess, who called back over her shoulder as she carried her tray into the kitchen, 'And when you ask her ladyship about going to see the flower garden, ask too if you can bring Mary to watch the seine-fishing on the beach tomorrow. She'd like that, I'm sure — all the nets being rowed out, and then the catch of fish on the beach. I'll be there, and I'll bring Bobby. Perhaps they might play together. And I expect you'll see Matt.' Matt, a trawlerman, had been my childhood sweetheart, but no longer.

'What a good idea,' I said quickly. 'Hope to see you then, Jess. Well, goodbye for now. We must run or we'll be late for luncheon. And I don't want to get into Mrs Frobisher's bad books, do I?'

Jess's laughter followed me down the street as she called back, 'Why not ask Mr Daniel? I bet if you give him a big smile he won't say no! I'm sure he likes a pretty girl!'

I laughed as I followed, taking Mary's hand in mine and listening to her chatter about the flowers as we walked back towards the Esplanade. But Jess's words stayed in my mind. Was Mr Daniel known for liking pretty girls, then? Somehow the idea displeased me. But then I told myself I was only a nursemaid and had no reason to worry about what Mr Daniel did with his life. I should be concentrating on making Mary happy, and keeping my new position.

Mrs Frobisher was pleased with the flowers and, after a pause of hard thinking, nodded when I asked permission to visit the flower seller's cottage sometime, and agreed to our watching the seine-fishing. 'But don't let Mary get wet. We don't want her catching cold, do we?' she said in her very firm voice. And I found myself wondering who was bringing up Mary — her father, or her grandmother?

3

Mary was excited as, after tea, we walked down to the beach where the fishing boats were drawn up, close to the men busy with nets as they prepared for the evening's seine-fishing. 'Will Becky be there?' she asked, as she skipped along beside me.

'Perhaps.'

But I was wondering if the idea of telling stories about this fictional little girl who lived on a boat had been a good idea. I was realizing more every day that Mary had a big and lively imagination, as well as lots of energy, so possibly it would be best to start a new story with a quieter adventure for her to think about. I foresaw problems with Mrs Frobisher, who clearly wanted Mary to be one of those children who was seen but not heard. And yet Mr Daniel, I was sure, had other thoughts

about his only and much-loved daughter.

For the first time I realised that this situation as nursemaid wasn't as easy as I had imagined it would be when I applied for it. But it was rewarding to have Mary's quick attention, and perhaps her growing love — she had held her face up for a kiss when I tucked her into bed last night. Now I thought hard about the elegant, beautifully furnished house that the Frobisher family lived in and slowly began to understand that the one missing thing in it was love. Just as it was in my own life. So what could I do about it?

But then Mary had pulled away from my hand and was rushing down the beach and stopping beside the boat, which two men were pulling down into the water. 'Let me help!' she cried, but Matt, smiling at me as he shook his head, led her back to me.

'Keep an eye on the little maid,' he said. 'Water's cold and tide's going out — dangerous for little 'uns.'

She tried to pull away, but I was ready for it, and held on to her very securely. She looked at me and pouted. 'I want to go and see the boat, Lily; see if it's like the one Becky lives in. Let me go!'

I shook my head, but smiled at her fierce expression. 'You must stay here with me, Mary, away from the water. Just think if you fell in!'

She frowned, but I felt her small hand grow easier in mine. 'If I did, I'd swim away. I want an adventure, like Becky has.'

By now the rowers had pushed the boat into the water and were starting to row out from the shore, pulling the huge net after them, while a group of men stayed on the beach holding its other end. I had seen this happening many times, and it was a fascinating sight to watch the huge shoal of fish being entrapped as the net was rowed in a wide circle and then pulled back to the shore. I glanced down at Mary and saw by her expression that she was

enjoying all she saw. And then Jess arrived with her brother Bobby. We introduced the children to each other, and Bobby grinned at Mary.

'If you like, you can help me load up my little cart when they gets the fish in. Will you?' he said.

Mary's huge smile was her answer, and I watched then as the two children became busy with Bobby's little cart, cleaning it out and making it ready for the catch. Jess and I sat with our backs to the sea wall, watching them; and although I enjoyed the warmth and the interesting scene, I was ready to run to the rescue if Miss Mary got too excited.

The men at the oars were shouting, encouraging, as they rowed. Matt's voice echoed back to us on the shore. 'Pull, pull! C'mon, b'ys. Harder!' And slowly the two ends of the net came together in a half-circle as the rowers touched shore again, meeting the men on the beach hauling at the far end of the net. Then the net was heaved out of the water, landing on the wet sand, with

fading sunlight falling on the wriggling mass of fish still within.

Mary and Bobby were excited, running down to the water's edge to look at the catch, so Jess and I got up and ran, too, careful to catch hold of the children's jacket edges in case they might fall into the heaving mound of fish.

'I want one to take back to Grandmother! Give me a fish, please!' Mary cried wildly. Bobby turned to her.

'You have to wait till we gets 'em out of the net. But we'll give the men a hand, shall we?'

It was all Jess and I could to keep hold of them! What a sight it was — the gleaming, wriggling mass, fish slowly being dug out of the net and put into buckets and baskets, little carts and prams, and even spread-out sheets. As the work came to an end, Jess took Bobby's little cart and helped both children to dip into the fish and fill it up.

I stood beside Mary and saw how her

face shone with pleasure as she dug her hands in, helping to fill the cart. And I began to smell fish all around us. I turned to Jess.

'I must take Mary home and change her clothes before Mrs Frobisher knows what she's been doing,' I said. 'But haven't they had fun? I can remember, as a child, the thrill of helping unload the catch the seine-fishers brought in — so in a way, it's good for Mary to do it, don't you think?'

And Jess grinned at me as she brushed scales off Bobby's jacket. 'I think the little maid needs some excitement in her life. The nanny she had before you was very strict and quiet, by all accounts. So don't worry about this adventure; it's doing her good.'

*   *   *

And then she turned away, for Matt had come up to me, suggesting we go out one evening. I was glad when Jess

interrupted, saying she was going to take Bobby — and his cart — onto the pier for an ice-cream before going home.

Jess called goodbye as they walked away down the beach, and it was all I could do to stop Mary running after them. Her glowing smile faded, and she looked at me with the pout I was slowly becoming used to. 'Why can't we go too, Lily? I don't want to go home yet.'

I wiped her hands with my handkerchief, tidied her blown-about hair and fixed her hat more securely. 'Perhaps another day we'll go on the pier, Mary. But we must go home now. Handling all those fish has made your clothes very dirty and smelly and you need a wash. Come along.'

And I took her hand firmly in mine and didn't really notice that she kept her other hand in her jacket pocket. If only I had done so.

★   ★   ★

When we returned to Three the Esplanade, I managed to get Mary through the back door without anyone seeing her and hoped that I could change her clothes and clean her up before bedtime, when she always went down to say goodnight to her father and her grandmother. I was just turning to close the door behind us when her hand slipped out of mine and she was running into the hall and towards the drawing room.

'Mary! Come back!'

If she heard me, she paid no attention, but instead opened the door and went into the room with me racing along behind, trying to stop any terrible shocks that she might give Mrs Frobisher, who sat in her chair by the window, embroidery frame on her lap and right hand holding a threaded needle.

She gave Mary a tight smile. 'Good gracious, what are you doing here? Not bed time yet, surely?'

And then I watched her expression

change, her eyes widen, and her mouth tighten as Mary stood at her side, pulling a glistening, smelly fish out of her jacket pocket. 'It's a present for you, Grandmother. You can get Cook to fry it for your supper, can't you?'

I stepped up behind her and tried to lower her arm holding the shining object, but no, she had put it in Mrs Frobisher's lap, and there it lay, already staining the embroidery, and filling the room with its sea-fresh smell.

I shut my eyes and listened to my heart racing. However had I allowed this to happen? Oh, Mary, Mary, so contrary, was there nothing you would stop at? But no good to think such things, for Mrs Frobisher was on the war path, pushing the fish from her lap, wiping her embroidery, wringing her hands, and looking at her grandchild with shocked, narrowed eyes. 'Go away, you terrible child! Miss Ross,' she said, looking at me with anger all over her face, 'take her to the nursery and put her in the bath

and scrub her clean and change her clothes *at once*. And put this . . . this . . . ' The fish was pushed down to the floor. ' . . . in the rubbish bin. Really, I can't imagine how you allowed this to happen. Mary, go upstairs with Miss Ross — no, never mind the fish — *just go.*'

Poor Mary looked at her irate grandmother with an expression of surprise and hurt. 'But it's a present . . . '

'Just go, child!'

Slowly, Mary turned and looked at me. I bent, picked up the fish in one hand, took Mary's hand in the other and firmly led her towards the door. 'Open it, please, Mary. And don't argue.'

Mrs Frobisher's voice followed me, high and angry. 'Miss Ross, kindly come down here before dinner. My son will have to be told about this misdemeanor, and will no doubt have something to say to you.'

Silently I nodded, and Mary and I left the room. I could see that, by now,

she understood she had done some-thing really wrong, so obediently she came with me. We reached the kitchen, gave the fish to a very surprised Mrs Hodge, and then went up to the nursery, her feet dragging as I pulled her along, finally coming to a stop by the fireside, where I undressed her and prepared her bath.

Only later, as I wrapped her in a warm towel, did she seem to escape from her guilty feelings. 'I'm sorry Grandmother was cross, Lily. But it was lovely on the beach. Can Bobby and I play again tomorrow?'

I had no idea whether I would be here tomorrow after this awful business, so I said quietly, 'Let's wait and see what tomorrow's like, shall we, Mary? There may be other things we need to do.' Like finding another nursemaid, I thought miserably, and hugged her tightly before she put on her night clothes and sat at the table, waiting for the housemaid to come up with her supper.

And then, somehow, I managed to dream up a story about Becky, who lived on the boat in the harbour. But this time it was a carefully managed story about her being a very good little girl, doing nothing naughty, and so pleasing all her family and friends.

Mary ate up her supper of soup, bread and sago, and then, before getting into bed, said, 'I hope Becky will do something interesting tomorrow. She's a bit dull today, isn't she?'

I wiped the smile off my face, and said sternly, 'Every little girl must be dull some of the time, for adventures can worry their families, Mary. And we don't want that, do we?'

As she slipped into bed, she looked at me with a very serious expression. 'No, Lily,' she said. 'But didn't you have adventures when you were small?'

I didn't know how to answer, for certainly I had had adventures which had left Aunt Edie shouting at me. But Mary must learn to behave, so I said, as I turned out the gas and prepared to go

downstairs to see Mrs Frobisher and Mr Daniel and learn my fate, 'Perhaps I'll tell you some of them tomorrow, Mary. Now off to sleep, and have sweet dreams.'

I tidied myself and walked slowly downstairs, aware that my own dreams were decidedly not very sweet.

* * *

I entered the drawing room feeling very nervous. At once, I saw Mr Daniel standing by the large window, close to his mother's chair. He looked across the room at me, and smiled slightly. 'Come in, Lily. Sit down — no need to keep standing.'

Did I imagine it, or did his straight mouth lift into a hint of amusement? Surely not. But his voice, as he continued, was light and hardly full of the anger and blame I expected.

'I used to watch the seine-fishing myself as a lad,' he went on, and I saw his eyes light up. 'Exciting, isn't it? And

41

I daresay you watched it, too, when you were younger.'

'Yes,' I whispered, memories of Matt returning.

'It's something every local child should see. So I don't blame you for taking Mary out to watch. But, of course, from what my mother tells me, it's Mary herself who is to blame most for what happened next.'

I was right; his smile was broader, but gradually it faded as he continued.

'Unfortunately, my daughter is lively — perhaps too lively? And so, with the slightest amount of freedom, she finds adventures for herself. There have been one or two in the past, but Nanny Brooks did not take her to places where such things might occur. Now, with her new nurse, she obviously thinks she has more freedom. Wouldn't you agree, Lily?'

What could I say? Of course I agreed. But Mrs Frobisher was frowning at me, and I feared her influence on Mr Daniel would at once make him say I

was no good at my job, and so must leave.

I cleared my throat and tried to sound efficient and apologetic. 'I'm sorry, Mr Daniel, that I let go of Mary's hand for a few moments. It's me who is to blame, and I don't think she should be punished for taking advantage of what was my fault.'

There was silence, and I felt Mrs Frobisher's cold eyes fixing on my face. I tried to sound even more apologetic as I continued. 'And of course, Mrs Frobisher, I will arrange to have your embroidery cleaned; and I will sponge down your stained dress, if you will allow me to.'

She waited a long, long nerve-stretching moment before answering in her chilly voice. 'Certainly you will do both those things, Miss Ross. That is — ' And here she looked at Mr Daniel, her eyes clearly challenging him. ' — if my son thinks you are capable of continuing as Mary's nurse-maid. For I fear you have given no sign

of proving yourself up to the position so far.'

My heart raced even faster. So here it was — my dismissal. However would I explain to Mary? And to Aunt Edie? And Jess? What would they think of me? And would I ever obtain another situation in future? For clearly, Mrs Frobisher would give me no reference.

Nervously, I looked at Mr Daniel, waiting for his nice smile to disappear, and to hear his voice become unfriendly as he dismissed me.

4

But instead he walked to a wing chair within the bay window, sat down, and then smiled at his mother. 'I fear I must disagree with you, Mama, that Lily is not suitable for the position she holds. For I truly think young Mary has many lessons to learn about behaving herself and not worrying people with her adventures. And without doubt Lily is the person to teach her. She's young, Mary already is growing fond of her, and her knowledge of the town is invaluable, for she can take Mary about and teach her many things. So, Lily — ' He half-turned and looked across the room at me. ' — I propose to make your contract a permanent one. That is, if you would like me to do so?'

I could find no words, for my heart was pumping and I could not completely believe what he had said. But

there was an expression of sincerity and warmth on his face telling me that he meant every word, which slowly returned me to calmness and more sensible thoughts. Small drifts of pleasure began to fill me. He thought I was a good nursemaid. Mary might grow to love me. We could still have adventures, but I would know the sensible places to take her for such little outings. And suddenly my mind was floating. I got up, unable to keep still any longer, and went swiftly across the room until I stood in front of him.

'Oh, thank you, Mr Daniel. Thank you . . . and I will do my very best with Mary.' My voice was unsteady and I could only smile and smile.

He rose, looking down at me with his deep eyes and that kindliness which I had seen before and enjoyed, so much a part of him when he was not looking tired and overworked. 'So that's decided, and I'm very pleased you wish to stay with us. Tomorrow you must come to the emporium and I

will arrange for you to be fitted for some suitable clothes; what do nannies wear? I'm sure you know better than I do!' He was laughing, and I laughed with him.

'A dark dress, Mr Daniel, that's important — and perhaps a big white apron, and a cap . . . '

Here I was interrupted by Mrs Frobisher's harsh voice cutting in. 'Daniel, leave it to your manageress to dress Lily appropriately for her situation. But certainly she must have a dark coat and hat for outdoor walks. I must insist that, when out with Mary, she looks a really professional nanny, for at the moment . . . ' She bit off the final words but I guessed what they might have been.

I felt her eyes on me and coloured. So she hadn't approved of my old clothes; but now it would be different. And I felt a new confidence, helping me stand up straighter and speak more easily. I would indeed prove to her that I could be a professional nanny.

'Thank you, Mr Daniel. And I apologise, Mrs Frobisher, for not dressing to the standard you require.' Childhood memories suddenly surged through me. 'You see, I come from a family that has to count every penny it earns, and clothes are the last things we spend our money on. But in future I shall be more the nanny you expect, and I hope that will please you.'

The words rushed out before I could stop them, and I saw from her expression that she was shocked — and extremely displeased. But suddenly I wasn't sorry for what I had said. It was the truth, and I knew myself to be a truthful girl. I met her stare, and smiled as sweetly as I could manage. And beside me, Mr Daniel said gently, 'Well said, Lily. We understand your position and I hope that dressing more professionally tomorrow will give you pleasure, for you deserve it. And I'm sure my mother realises this.' He looked at her — a long, unsmiling look which slowly she returned with a nod

of the head and a grudging slight smile.

'Indeed, Lily,' she said at last, 'my son is right. You are a good worker, and so you deserve to improve your status in life.'

For a stretching moment we all stayed still and silent, and I knew I had said enough, as had Mr Daniel, let alone his difficult mother. I walked to the door, turned, smiled and said politely, 'I will go and see that Mary is sleeping soundly. And thank you for allowing me to continue in my position as nanny. Good night, Mrs Frobisher, Mr Daniel.' And I left the room.

⋆   ⋆   ⋆

The next morning I told Mary I had a different adventure for her — we would visit her father's emporium and she would spend a little time in the toy department with one of the sales ladies. Her face lit up and she became excited, so much so that I had to sit her down

and look at a book after breakfast until she was quieter.

We put on our coats and hats and walked along the Esplanade. The sea was calm this morning, with small lacy waves washing up onto the sandy beach. I suggested that another morning we might walk along the beach and look for shells.

Mary jumped about and held my hand very tightly. She smiled up at me. 'I would like that, Lily. Is it what Becky does sometimes? And what shells does she find, I wonder?'

I went back into my childhood and remembered finding shells with Matt, and what fun it was. 'Winkles,' I said, smiling down at her. 'And limpets, and mussels, and razor shells, and sometimes lovely mother-of-pearl. We'll go and look tomorrow, Mary.'

She skipped along beside me, and then we walked into the town and entered the emporium. The shop worker, Mr Rowden, greeted us warmly and led Mary to the toy department,

where a sales lady said she would very much enjoy showing Mary all the latest toys. Then Mr Rowden said, 'I will ask our manageress, Mrs Burton, to take you into the dress department, so please follow me, Miss Ross.'

He left me in the large room upstairs, full of manikins wearing lovely dresses and sales girls busy dressing the models, and then Mrs Burton appeared from her little office at the back of the room.

'Welcome, Miss Ross,' she said with a smile. 'Mr Daniel has told me just what you require, so if you come with me you can see what I have selected for you to try on.'

What a wonderful time that was! Several dark dresses were laid on the chair beside the big pier mirror, and Mrs Burton drew a curtain so that I could try them on.

'You have a very good figure,' she said. 'Slim, and yet tall enough to carry off lovely gowns. Mr Daniel has asked us to try the this dark dress and see if it

fits you.' Her first choice was slightly too big and fell off my shoulders, but the next one might have been made for me. It fitted perfectly. I looked at my reflection and thought how smart it was, dark green fine wool and beautifully cut, and made me look much more sure of myself.

Then Mrs Burton called in one of the sales girls, who brought in some dark hats. 'Mr Daniel said you probably needed a nurse's cap, but he thought perhaps a smart hat would be more suitable . . . ' She arranged the fine straw hat with its wide brim and well-fitting crown on my head, and as I looked, I thought I saw a new Lily Ross. Surely this wasn't the seaside girl who helped clear up Aunt Edie's bakery? Who went on walks with Matt when she was younger, and picked up shells on the beach? No, I saw a young woman dressed elegantly, if plainly, but who stood tall and looked capable and sure of herself. What an exciting moment.

Mrs Burton nodded her head. 'I expect you would like to wear the dress and the hat straight away, wouldn't you, Miss Ross? We will send your other clothes to the house later today. Oh, and Mr Daniel said he would like to see you before you left. Follow me and I'll take you to his office.'

I was surprised; why would Mr Daniel want to see me? Had he got orders for me to take Mary somewhere in particular? But I went with Mrs Burton into the little room where he was sitting at his desk, and at once he swivelled around and got up.

'Miss Ross . . . ' He stopped, and I wondered if the dress was wrong, or if the hat made me look too dressy for a nanny. But then he slowly smiled, and I saw that warm friendliness smooth out the lines on his lean face. 'Why, Lily, you look wonderful,' he said slowly. 'Are you pleased with the outfit? Do you think it's suitable for your position?'

I took a big breath then said a bit unsteadily, 'If you're pleased, Mr

Daniel, then I am, too. And thank you so much for these lovely clothes. I shall wear them with pride.' And I meant it; for I felt young Lily Ross, a bit of a wild child, always at odds with Aunt Edie, had become a more mature and sensible young woman. Thanks to him — and Mary.

Then I remembered Mary, in the toy department. So I said quickly, 'I will go and find Mary now, and we'll finish our morning walk. Thank you again, Mr Daniel.' And I left his office, with him still standing there. I thought I felt his eyes watching me as I went, but I told myself that was my imagination, and all because I was so pleased with myself. I knew I must now get back into being a sensible nanny, and thinking of how to amuse Mary next.

She stared when she saw me, and stopped pushing a model pram up and down the toy department. 'Goodness, Lily, don't you look different! What a lovely hat!'

'I'm glad you like it — your

grandmother will think I look more like a nanny now!'

Mary put her hand in mine as we went downstairs and back into the town. 'You're a much nicer nanny than Nanny Brooks,' she said, and I gasped a bit, but what is it they say — ? Out of the mouths of babes ... So perhaps I was filling my role quite well.

We walked back towards the Esplanade along the seafront. And again Mary asked about shells. 'I think shells would look very pretty with flowers, don't you, Lily?' she asked.

I said, 'Yes, I do. And that reminds me, perhaps I could ask your papa to allow us to drive out to the flower lady's cottage and see her garden?'

'Oh yes, that would be lovely,' she said, and then suddenly pulled away from me, running towards the pier, just a stone's throw away from us. In vain did I hurry after her, calling her to stop and wait for me; but of course she didn't, and by the time I reached the pier she was already through the

entrance gate and skipping along towards the café at the very end, where the steamers came in.

Here she stopped and looked back at me. 'Hurry up, Lily,' she called as I approached. 'We can have some lemonade, can't we?' And I thought, why not? At least she'd be sitting down for ten minutes.

'Very well, Mary,' I said, 'but you must sit still while we're here. Now, would you like a biscuit with your lemonade?'

The waitress came up, smiling, and took our order. Then, before leaving us, she said, 'I hope you saw the posters that are advertising the dance competition? They're all along the rails — you'll see them as you go back, I expect.'

Mary looked at her, then at me, and her blue eyes were wide. 'Dancing? I love dancing! Can I come, Lily?'

I undid her coat as the sun was pouring in through the big windows. It was lovely sitting there in the warmth, with the gulls screaming outside,

following the fishing boats into the harbour. I was very full of my new clothes, and for a moment Mary's request meant nothing. I smiled and said, 'I expect so,' and then thought about something else.

But Mary got up from her chair and without a word, started dancing around the room. She hummed to herself, and I thought I heard nursery tale tunes, but suddenly I realised how shocking it was that Miss Mary Frobisher was dancing in public in the pier café! And of course, there were other people sitting there drinking their chocolate and tea and coffee, and they all looked as she whirled past their tables.

I got up in a hurry, following her around as she twirled and spun, and then caught her by the back of her jacket and said, 'Mary, you must stop at once! This is no way to behave, and certainly this is no place for you to practise your dancing with all these people looking on! Come and sit down

and drink your lemonade, and then we must go home.'

I took her back to her chair, and she sat down, frowning and even sulking for a few moments, until the waitress arrived with the jug of lemonade and my cup of coffee and smiled down at her as she placed the cup on the table. Before she left us, she looked at me and nodded. 'The manager saw the little girl dancing, and hopes very much that she will enter the competition next week — Friday evening at five-thirty. Will you bring her?'

I sat in silence, not replying, although of course Mary did. 'To dance with other people? Oh how lovely! Yes, Lily and I will come and dance — and we'll wear our best dresses!'

My mind did a somersault. How was I going to prevent her doing this?

5

As we walked along the Esplanade, a voice hailed me from the beach — and there was Matt, looking at me with wide eyes. 'Why, Lily, what's come over you? Someone left you a fortune, have they? My word, you look splendid!' He stopped and so Mary and I paused, too.

I felt awkward. Matt and I had gone to school together and been friends ever since. But now I knew I was working in a place where he would have no welcome, being just a fisherman. Not that Mr Daniel would be unpleasant, but I guessed Mrs Frobisher would have no time for such a working man. Expecially if he smelt of fish — which Matt certainly did.

I took hold of Mary's hand even more firmly — who knew what she might do with a friendly fisherman to encourage her? — and said, 'This is my

nursemaid's uniform, Matt. I have this good situation looking after Mr Frobisher's little girl, you see.' And I smiled down towards Mary.

Matt bent down and I remembered how good he always was with animals and small children. He was grinning at Mary and offering her a shell he took out of his pocket. 'Like this, would you, maid? Put it to your ear and you'll hear the waves coming up the beach. Maybe Lily'll take you beach-combing one day, and goodness knows what you'll find then.'

'Matt, please don't encourage her — yes, we'll go looking for shells, but I don't want her to try and do it on her own.' I frowned at him and shook my head so that he would understand. As he stood up straight, and Mary seemed busy listening to the shell, I stepped nearer and whispered, 'She likes to run off and have adventures! Don't encourage her!'

He nodded. 'Course I won't. But a maid with spirit like her, she'll want to

do exciting things. So how about a boat trip with me one morning when the tide's right?'

I didn't know what to say. Yes, I'd love to spend time with Matt like I used to, but with Mary at my side everything was different. I think he saw my answer on my face, for he stepped away and his voice was suddenly colder and not so friendly.

'But I guess you don't want to do simple things like that now, not now that you're part of the Frobisher family. Well, always nice to see you, Lily — and Mary — but I gotta go now. So goodbye.' And he marched away ahead of us, quickly disappearing around the corner towards the beach.

Mary looked up at me, disappointment all over her face. 'Where's he gone?'

'To see to his boat, I expect. The fishermen keep them pulled up on the river beach. But it was kind of him to give you that shell, wasn't it?'

She held it in her free hand as we

walked along and looked at it. 'Yes. It's lovely. And I want to find some more — can we . . . ?'

I interrupted quickly. 'Yes, Mary, we'll go looking for shells one morning, but now we have to get home for luncheon. Come along.' I almost pulled her into the gateway of Number Three. Only when we were at home did I feel safe. And I was beginning to think that Mary, an intelligent child, was busily planning things which I knew I would never allow her to do. So taking her up to the nursery and preparing for luncheon was a safeguard, and I was relieved to be doing it.

At luncheon Mrs Frobisher seemed in a friendlier mood. She smiled at me as the meal ended and said, 'You look much more professional now, Lily. Very nice indeed. And I understand the shop will deliver your winter coat and some spare dresses very soon. So now, what are you and Mary proposing to do this afternoon, I wonder?'

I thought about the flower lady and

her invitation, and at once turned towards Mr Daniel, who was standing in the big bay window, looking down at the Esplanade outside, and I said quickly, 'Mary is very eager to take up the invitation of the flower lady, Mr Daniel. Would it be possible for us to be driven there in your trap this afternoon? We wouldn't stay long, but Mary would enjoy seeing the flowers, and it would be another useful interest for her to know about gardens.'

He turned and looked at me for what seemed a long moment. I felt embarrassed, but there was no need, for finally he smiled and said, 'What a good idea. Yes, Eddie shall drive you both to wherever this garden is — not far, I suppose?'

'On the outskirts of town, the flower lady said. I think it's one of the cottages on Bishop Road. Only a mile or two.' I was pleased to see the way he looked at me — easily, warm, and almost as if we were friends and not just employer and nursemaid. And that made me add,

'Perhaps Mary will think about study-ing flowers and painting them.'

His smile was infectious. 'And so you can keep her in the nursery, is that it? No more dangerous adventures for you to deal with, Nurse Lily?' His voice was light, and amusement shone in his eyes.

I felt my cheeks colour, but I had the sense to reply equally lightly. 'No, Mr Daniel, not just that, because I enjoy Mary's little adventures. But I, too, love flowers, and will really enjoy learning more about them.'

He nodded, then turned to his mother and said, 'And so, before you leave for London, Mama, you can have the pleasure of knowing that young Mary is to start studying. Will that please you?'

Mrs Frobisher walked to his side, put her hand on his arm and smiled. 'You love to joke, Daniel. But yes, I do think the child needs some more serious education than just . . . ' She glanced over her shoulder at me, a pointed look. ' . . . bringing dead fish home and

ruining my second-best gown.'

I said quickly, 'The dry cleaner will deliver the gown tomorrow, Mrs Frobisher, and I trust it will be as good as new.'

She nodded, turned away from Mr Daniel and walked towards the door. 'Yes, you've been very good about getting it cleaned, Lily. And it will be here in time to accompany me to London when I go to stay with my younger son, Paul, at the end of this week.' She paused in the doorway, looked at me again, and gave me a warmer smile than I'd ever seen before. 'My son works abroad, so this is a special few weeks in London where we can be together again.' Her smile beamed and again, she nodded, then left the room and I heard her ascend the stairs.

I looked at Mr Daniel, who was watching with a slightly bemused look on his thin face. He turned to me. 'My mother has her favourites, as you no doubt understand,' he said drily. And

then, sighing, he added, 'I'll tell Eddie to bring the trap around at two-thirty. Will that give you time to get Mary ready for her flower outing?'

I said, 'Yes, thank you, Mr Daniel, and we'll be back here for tea.'

'But I shan't.' For a moment I thought he was going to add something, but then he straightened his shoulders and said, 'Time to return to the emporium, I think.' And he left me alone in the dining room.

★   ★   ★

Eddie had the trap ready for us after luncheon, and we drove steadily through the town and along the road towards the next village. I had asked him to stop briefly at the Seaspray Café so that I could ask Jess the flower lady's address, and she looked at me with what seemed to be admiration as she said, 'Goodness, Lily, don't you look smart? Birthday present in advance, was it?'

'Of course not. This is my uniform, Jess. And anyway, no one knows anything about my birthday.'

Mary pulled at my arm. 'When is your birthday, Lily? Can we have a cake, and a party?'

I grinned at Jess and shook my head. 'There, see what you've started! My birthday is next week, Mary, and yes, I expect I'll buy a cake that we can share.' Suddenly I thought it would be a chance to call in at Aunt Edie's bakery and let her see how I was getting on. But that must wait. Now we must drive out to the flower lady's home called Rose Cottage on Bishop Road.

Back in the trap I told Eddie what to look out for, and soon he halted the pony outside a small white-washed cottage with a little garden in front and a white painted gate. 'I'll hitch Duchess to that tree, Miss Lily, and wait for you. The old gel can eat some grass, and I'll sit down and have a smoke.' He smiled as Mary and I climbed down and went towards the gate.

'I can open it!' Mary's small hands were wrestling with the rather rusty latch. Suddenly the front door opened and the flower lady looked at us with surprise, but then smiled and came to greet us.

'Why, 'tis Lily and Miss Mary — come in, come in . . . ' She opened the door wider and stood aside to let us enter.

Mary went ahead of me, standing still in the small room opening up before us and looking around her. 'Why is it so dark?' she asked, and I shook my head at her.

'It's because this is a little house, not so big as your home,' I told her. 'But isn't it warm and lovely?' I looked at the flower lady, who stood there, smiling at us. 'Please forgive Mary's lack of manners,' I said. 'She's always so interested in what she sees that I fear she says whatever comes into her mind.' And turning to Mary, I said, 'Try and keep quiet for a few minutes, Mary. Just look around, and remember everything

so that you can tell your papa when you get home.'

She didn't answer but nodded, and then straightaway went to the window at the back of the room. 'There's a garden!' she cried, looking back at me. 'Can I go out there, please, Lily? I promise I won't do anything naughty . . .'

The flower lady looked at me, her eyebrows raised, so I said, 'Mary is inclined to want adventures, but she'll be safe enough out there, won't she?'

'Of course she will. There's a little stream at the bottom, but it's only inches deep, and we'll keep our eyes on her.' She paused, and I could see her thinking what to do next. Then she said, 'Would you like to sit down by the fire? I'll make a cup of tea, and then we'll take it into the garden and see what Miss Mary is doing.'

'That would be lovely, thank you,' I said, and sat down in a creaky cane chair by the open fire, where a blackened kettle stood on a trivet over the flames.

She pushed the trivet further over the flames and added a few dry sticks to the blaze. Then she looked at me, pulled out a stool and sat down opposite, saying, 'I was so hoping you would come to see me. I've been waiting every day . . . '

We looked at each other, and I thought she looked slightly fearful. I said, 'Why do you say that? We don't know one another, do we? So why . . . ?'

She broke in, cutting off my words, her voice unsteady. 'Because I have something to tell you, Lily.' Her eyes were huge and I saw they were full of tears. She repeated, almost under her breath, 'Lily. My little Lily. So you're here at last, with me, and perhaps I can make up for everything I did back then . . . oh, I do hope so.'

I sat up straighter and the chair creaked as if in pain. 'What do you mean? Why, I don't even know your name. Who are you?' I heard my voice rising and wondered at the sudden tightening inside me. I had a feeling

that this was an important moment in my life, and yet who could it be? It was just an afternoon visit to keep Mary amused, after all.

The flower lady sat very straight on her stool and looked into my eyes. 'Dorothy is my name,' she said slowly, 'but everyone calls me Dodie, and I am called Ross, like you. You see . . . ' She stopped and I watched the tears in her eyes begin to trickle down her lined face.

I didn't know what to say, or to think. So we shared the same surname. But we didn't know one another — did we? It must just be a strange and unexpected coincidence. And yet . . . instinct suddenly knotted inside me, and I waited with a feeling of breathlessness for what I guessed she was going to tell me.

Dodie Ross reached out her hands and held them, trembling just in front of me, as she said, so quietly I could hardly hear her, 'Dear Lily, you're the baby I left, nineteen years ago, with my

sister Edie.' The catch in her voice deepened. 'I'm your mother, Lily.'

A great pain surged through me then, and quick anger came to hide it so that I couldn't stop the words rushing out. 'No,' I cried. 'I don't believe you! You can't be my mother — and even if you are, I don't want anything to do with you!'

6

Her hands dropped, and she looked at me in horror. 'But you mustn't say that! Pete and I loved you, of course we did; but it was hard to find work, and so I did what I thought was the best — leaving you with Edie, who looked after you better than I could have done, being on the road like we were, going from town to town looking for work. Edie gave you a home, she loved you . . . '

I sprang to my feet and looked down at her, all my feelings rushing out in rapid words. 'No, she never loved me! She made use of me — and it's only now that I've got this good situation that I'm starting to live properly. I don't want to be your daughter because you never looked after me!'

She rose and her voice steadied. 'How could I? A tiny baby, and Pete

and me earning our few pennies by digging gardens, cutting lawns, planting bushes, and sleeping in barns, or wherever we could find shelter — what could I have done with you while we worked so hard? You shouldn't blame me, Lily — and you should be glad that we've met up again. I know I am. Oh, my lovely girl, I've thought so much about you, and longed and longed to know if you were all right . . . And now we're here, together . . . '

It wasn't what I had expected to hear, and slowly my anger died away. We stood in that little room, with the fire crackling beside us and the scent of roses on the table drifting all around. We looked at each other and I saw a hesitant, pleading smile spread across her face. My heart ached. What could I do but reply to it?

I put out a hand and she took it; hers was strong and calloused, but so warm and loving that I could only say, 'I'm sorry. I don't want to hurt you, Dodie . . . Mother. But it's been a shock

discovering who you are — who I am . . . ' I paused, my head churning, then added, 'So I think Mary and I will go now. I need time to think, you see . . . '

'Yes, of course. You're right.' Her hand dropped but the smile grew, and she moved to the door into the garden, saying over her shoulder, 'Mary can pick some flowers before you go — but won't you wait and have that cup of tea I was going to make? Please, Lily — just five minutes for a cup of tea?'

I followed her into the garden, and the beauty all around surprised me. For this was a garden full of many sorts of flowers, and behind the little stream flowing at the bottom stood a clump of graceful trees. It struck me that nature is more beautiful than we ever really notice — and that Mary and I were lucky to be here. There was a sense of peace. So I smiled at her and said quietly, 'Thank you, yes, we'd love a cup of tea. I'll go and talk to Mary while you make it.' I watched her nod

and saw her smile grow even bigger. Then she went back to the cottage and I heard the rattle of teacups being put on a tray.

Slowly, thoughtfully, I went in search of Mary. And found her up to her knees in the little stream that rippled over stones at the end of the garden. She was bending down, and straightened up when she head me say, 'Mary! Come out of that at once . . . Whatever are you doing?'

'Catching a tiny fish, Lily. I nearly got it but it slipped away, and it's hiding under that stone.' Again she bent down, but now I leant over the stream, got hold of her arm and pulled her out.

I heard all my upset come out in my voice as I said sharply, 'I can't leave you for a moment, can I? Mary, I think I shall have to put you on a lead next time we go out.'

By the time I had taken off her socks and shoes and dried her feet on my shawl, Dodie had come out with a tray, and we sat down together on a wooden

bench, with a small table in front of us. Mary saw the gingerbread biscuits and was delighted. 'Can I have one, please?' she asked.

I said firmly, 'You can if you may, Mary.' I caught Dodie's eye and we smiled together as if my hasty words were forgotten. But I knew they were not. Indeed, I foresaw that on returning to Number Three the Esplanade, and with Mary safely in bed this evening, I would sit in my bedroom and go over and over that horrible scene, and the past event which had caused it. But now, I had to think about Mary.

Dodie and I — she was not yet Mother in my mind — talked about trivial matters: picking a bunch of flowers to take home for the nursery; asking Mr Daniel to buy a flower book so that Mary could identify her favourites. Perhaps even buying a new paint box so that she could start copying one or two flowers. Anything to take our minds off what had just happened, I realised. When the teacups

were empty we picked the flowers and Mary pouted at having to leave this lovely garden. But Dorothy invited us to return, and so at last we were in the trap, driving slowly home with Mary sniffing her bunch of roses and lupins and cottage garden pinks.

That night, after a quiet supper in the nursery and another tale about Becky — this time helping to grow plants in her mother's garden and then finding a caterpillar on the leaf she held, which led to a lot of discovering how such creepy crawlies arrive there — Mary slept peacefully, and I sat on my bed in the moonlit room next door to hers, thinking about finding my mother and how I felt about it.

And the more I thought, the worse I felt. I reminded myself of the poor childhood I had as a result of being abandoned like that; not as if Aunt Edie gave me much love, although I did learn how hard even small girls must work to earn a living. I felt lonely, and heartsick. And then the tears I had so

far held back trickled down my face, and I indulged in being extremely sorry for myself.

I hadn't realised that my sobs were loud enough to be heard in the passage outside my room, but then there was a gentle knock on the door. Mrs Hodge, the cook, who slept a few doors away, peered in, looked at me with a worried expression and whispered, 'Why, Miss Lily, is something the matter? And can I help in some way?'

Her graying hair was plaited into a long pigtail and her robe was clutched over her rather large stomach, but I was so pleased to see her that I only thought of her kindness, and not the rather amusing figure she presented. At once I wiped my eyes and managed to smile at her. 'No, nothing really wrong, thank you, Mrs Hodge. Just thinking about the past . . . ' My voice broke, and she stepped into the room, putting her arms about me.

'Poor maid. I know, sometimes things that have happened come back to haunt

one. But there, you must try and get over them. You've got this good position, haven't you? And I think Miss Mary is fond of you, and Mr Daniel seems very pleased with all you do. You're on the way to being loved, I'm sure. So cheer up, do, my lover.'

Well, what could I do but wipe my face dry, put a smile there, and know that I would always remember this odd meeting in the night. 'You're so kind, Mrs Hodge,' I whispered back, 'and I shall be all right now. So do go back to your warm bed, and don't worry about me anymore, please.'

She took a step back, dropped her arms, and looked at me carefully. 'Very well. But if you ever need to talk to anyone, well, you can always come to me, maid. But I'll say goodnight now, and sleep well.' She nodded, smiled again, and disappeared back to her own room, leaving me ashamed of myself, and, as I slipped into bed, starting to count my blessings. I had a good position, a loving little girl to help bring

up, a kind employer, and now, of all things, my own mother back in my life. After a short while, I drifted off to sleep with a smile on my face.

Next day Mary kept asking me about my birthday, so reluctantly I told her, 'It's next Wednesday, and we'll go out and have tea at Jess's café, shall we?'

She smiled and said, 'And I'll give you a present. What would you like, Lily? I'll tell Papa and he'll buy you something nice. Like some sweets, I expect.'

That worried me. I didn't want Mr Daniel to think that he must do something about his nursemaid's birthday. Goodness, what would Mrs Frobisher say if she heard of that! But she was leaving for London in the afternoon, and I told Mary we would be at the front door to see her leave on her journey.

'Can we go to the station and see the train?' she asked.

'No, I don't think your grandmother would think that was the right thing to

do. We'll go and see Jess and Bobby, shall we? And perhaps call in at my aunt's bakery to order the cake I promised you.'

We saw Mrs Frobisher off from the front door, saw all her bags and hatboxes loaded into the cab taking her to the station, and then watched her and Mr Daniel drive off down the Esplanade with just a brief wave through the window as they left. I turned to Mary. 'Perhaps your grand-mother will send you a postcard when she's in London — something for you to watch for every day, Mary.'

'Yes,' she said solemnly. 'I'll wait for the postman in the morning.' Which left me wondering if I had raised her hopes. Would Mrs Frobisher think to do this? I hoped so.

That afternoon we walked to the Seaspray and found Jess busy ironing tablecloths in the room behind the café. She had Bobby with her, and at once he and Mary began playing with some small cake tins which they built up into

miniature houses, leaving me free to chat to Jess. I told her about Dodie telling me who she was, and how shocked I felt about it. I said, 'I told her I didn't want to see her again, which was a terrible thing to say. But, Jess, it was how I felt at the time. Was I wrong, do you think? And what should I do about it now?'

She put the iron back on the trivet on the range, and folded the clean cloth. 'Well,' she said after a thoughtful pause, 'you must have hurt her a lot. How did she take your answer?'

'Yes, she was hurt,' I admitted. 'But I don't think she realised just how much she had hurt *me*. My childhood wasn't all that happy.'

Jess stopped folding and looked across at me. Her hazel eyes looked directly into mine. 'But you got through it, didn't you, Lily? Your Aunt Edie brought you up to be a good, sensible, well-behaved girl — was it so bad, after all?'

And that made me think again. Yes,

of course she was right. I had no reason to blame Dodie — could I start calling her Mother now? No, it was too soon. But my thoughts were changing. I nodded at Jess. 'You're right, of course. And, actually, we parted on quite good terms. We had tea in the garden and promised to call again, so perhaps . . . '

Jess grinned her happy, warm smile. 'Perhaps you'll feel better soon, Lily. I do hope so. And I bet your mother — what did you call her, Dodie? — hopes so too. Now, can you help me fold this extra-big tablecloth?'

I did so, and then because Bobby and Mary were suddenly absent from the room, I jumped up and went to look for the adventurous pair. They were out in the street, and I had an awful fear that Bobby might take Mary down to the river beach. So I grabbed her hand, told Bobby to go back to the café, and firmly led my wriggling charge down towards Regent Row and Aunt Edie's bakery.

I felt a little nervous as we approached the shop front, wondering how my aunt would greet me — and Mary. We found her sitting quietly in the back room with a cup of tea at her side and her feet up on a stool. She got up as we entered, and I pulled Mary to my side as I said, 'Aunt Edie, I've brought Mary Frobisher to see you. I am her nursemaid, you see, and we thought we would like to come and visit the bakery — and you.' I bent down, whispering, 'Hold out your hand and smile, Mary, and be polite to Mrs Drew.'

Bless her, she did just that, and I could see my aunt's crusty face soften as she took the small hand in hers and smiled down at Mary. 'Well,' she said, 'how nice to have Miss Frobisher here. And perhaps she would like a piece of my newly baked bread? With some jam on it?'

Mary's face blossomed and she said, 'Yes, please! But we want to ask you to make a cake for Lily's birthday next

week — I think a chocolate cake would be lovely!'

Aunt Edie looked at me as she found a scrap of bread and spread a spoonful of raspberry jam on it, put it on a plate and then led Mary to the table by the fire. 'Sit down, maid, and eat up, and we'll think about the cake, shall we? But first I want to talk to your nanny — to Lily.' Then she turned to me and her smile faded. 'I have something to tell you,' she said in a quiet, almost secretive tone of voice, 'so you'd better sit down.'

7

I looked down at Mary, but she seemed too busy eating her bread to take any notice of me, so I said nervously, 'What is it, Aunt Edie? And is this the right place to talk about it? Perhaps if I came one evening when Mary has gone to bed . . . '

My aunt sat down again in her cane chair by the fire and looked at me with her usual determined expression. 'The maid's eating. She'll take no notice of us. And it'll only take a few minutes to tell you, but I feel you need to know.' She stopped, then put her handkerchief to her mouth, and went on. 'It's about your mother.' Again she stopped, and now I saw her mouth was trembling and her dark eyes were swimming. 'It's about Dodie, my little sister, who ran off and disappeared, leaving you here with me all those years ago. Well, now,

believe it or not, she's come back to the town; came here only the other day, asking after you.'

I felt something knot inside me. I wasn't sure if what Aunt Edie was saying was for the best or not. Perhaps if Dodie — Mother — really had been looking for me, I could feel better about things, because it sounded as if she needed to find me again. Yet I feared there would be fireworks from Aunt Edie. So I said carefully, 'Please tell me about it, Aunt Edie.'

'Well,' she said, shifting in her chair and fixing me with that dark gaze, 'this woman came into the bakery last week with baskets of flowers. I bought a bunch of pinks 'cause they smelt so nice, and then wondered what it was about her that seemed familiar. We looked at each other for a couple of moments, and then she smiled and said very quietly, 'Edie, it's been a long time, hasn't it? And I know I should have been in touch, but somehow life was hard and I just didn't — and then Pete

died and I was too upset to think straight. But now things are better, I'm more sensible, and I've rented this nice little cottage along Bishop Road, and I'm growing flowers to sell.''

Aunt Edie sniffed and wiped her nose and looked at me again. 'And then . . . then she asked me if I'd forgiven her . . . ' Her voice broke and she bent her head.

I kept quiet for a moment, seeing that she needed time to control her feelings. Which made me wonder what her reaction had been to that question. Slowly, I said, 'And have you, Aunt Edie, forgiven her?'

I watched her raise her head, once more wipe away the threatening tears, and then give me that straight, honest look which I knew I would always see in my mind whenever I thought of my childhood here in the bakery.

After another few seconds or so, she nodded slowly as she said, 'Difficult to say, maid. She left me with a child to bring up and no money. There was no

thought of how I would manage, no mention of if she was coming back again. She'd always been a bit wild, wanting her own way, and I guessed then that it might be a long time before we met again. So do you wonder that I hardened my heart then, and even now it's not as soft as it might be?'

I thought very hard. Of course, she was right. She had been treated badly, and now she was expected to forgive everything. Eventually I said, 'I understand your feelings, Aunt Edie. But perhaps you might find it in yourself to forgive your sister — my mother — because she's come to say she's sorry and she wants to try and make peace between you.'

As she had with me. My thoughts flew back to the flower garden and the little homely cottage where I had used hard words to Dodie, the mother who had come back looking for me. There was another long silence, with Mary finishing her bread and then getting up and coming to my side. 'Will you ask

Mrs Drew about the cake, Lily? And can we go and look at the boats on the river beach?'

Returning to the present, letting the confused thoughts fade away, I took her hand in mine and looked into her wide, sweet eyes and thought how different her life was from mine. For she had a family to love her; I had had only hard-hearted Aunt Edie, who bullied me into helping her with the never-ending work at the bakery. And then I heard again Jess's sensible words about how well I had grown up, and never mind the past. I had this excellent situation. I must think about the blessings that were mine now.

So I smiled at her and said, 'Yes, in a minute, Mary. But now let's ask Mrs Drew about the cake — a chocolate one, you suggested?'

I looked at Aunt Edie and saw she had a faint smile raising her straight, tight mouth as she said, 'A cake? Yes, of course, it's your birthday. I hadn't forgotten, you know. And the little maid

wants it to be chocolate, so that's what I'll make. Come again on Tuesday next week; it'll be ready then. And I hope you have a little party . . . '

Mary said quickly, 'Yes, we will! I've told Papa about it being Lily's birthday, and he said Wednesday is half-day at the emporium, so he'll be at home and we'll have a good time!'

I hoped my surprised and pleased expression wouldn't show to Aunt Edie, who was still looking at me with her dark, keen eyes. But what if she did see and wonder? I knew something extraordinary was happening inside me, warming my heart, hearing that Mr Daniel was ready to spend time helping me celebrate my birthday. And it felt too good to be kept to myself.

I was smiling as I jumped up, took Mary's hand and said, 'Well, goodbye, Aunt Edie, and I'll look forward to coming and collecting the cake. I remember the lovely ones you made when I lived with you . . . ' And then I stopped, for her expression had

changed. I realised I had reminded her of the past, and now she was faced with a problem in the present. But I knew she must resolve it herself, although I wished I could help in some way. So at the door I turned and smiled at her as I said gently, 'Next time I come we'll talk some more, Aunt Edie. And perhaps by then you might have changed your mind about forgiving . . . ' I paused. ' . . . my mother.' There, I had said it — not Dodie anymore, but who she really was: my mother.

I felt my blood racing as I acknowledged the truth, and knew tears were not far away, so I marched Mary down the street and felt the salt wind from the river beach chasing away those tears. Sand crunched under my feet, and all the childish woes I had felt in the past without a mother to love me faded away; here, with the sea and a safe position, and all the other blessings which I sensed were gathering around me, how could I be so silly as to let

those memories hurt me?

As we slowly walked along the beach and round to the Point where the ocean greeted the racing river, with Mary happily dancing alongside me, I forced myself to think about the fictional Becky, and what safe little adventure I could relate before we turned back to the Esplanade and home. I was just imagining Becky helping people with useful odd jobs, when Matt came up behind us and said, 'Lily! Just the girl I wanted to see. Now, maid, it's time you gave yourself some time off and spent some with me. How about that boat trip I suggested? I'm just off to bring in the crab pots. And your little girl can stay at home for once, surely? Here, Mary.' He bent down, fumbled in his pocket and produced a handful of shells, which he offered to her. 'Winkles, razor shells, limpets, even a rare pelican's foot — look, you can have them all and have fun with them, maid.'

Of course, Mary was delighted. She took all the shells from him, put them

down on the concrete path and then sat down beside them, fingering each one and looking up at him with a huge smile. 'Thank you. Oh, yes, they're lovely. Tell me the names again, please . . . '

I was shocked to see her sitting on the path and immediately tried to pull her up, but she glared at me and insisted on keeping her seat with hands carefully pulling the shells together. I had an awful thought of Mr Daniel coming home and seeing his daughter sitting there, but I had to smile. And it was that smile that encouraged Matt to say in a gentler, quieter tone, just for me to hear, 'Come on, Lily, just take an hour off so we can be together. Haven't had you to myself for a long time.'

I dithered. Yes, I would enjoy a short boat trip with Matt; we used to talk about so many things, and it might do me good to take a step back in time. And perhaps I could ask Mrs Hodge to take the shells from Mary and boil them up to remove the smell, and then

let her play in the kitchen sorting them until I came back.

I felt his hand on my arm, saw the hope in his brown eyes, and smiled. 'All right,' I said. 'I'll take Mary home and see she's looked after, then I'll be on the beach in half an hour. But we mustn't stay out there too long.'

★ ★ ★

Mrs Hodge laughed when I appeared in the kitchen with Mary clutching her smelly group of shells. 'Goodness, so she's doing what we all did as children, isn't she — and she'll probably be wanting to make a necklace of them once they'm boiled jest like you and me did as maids. Here, give them to me, Miss Mary, and I'll put them in this little pot to boil away that old fishy smell. And while you're waiting, you could help me cut out these biscuits I'm making.' She grinned at me. 'Go away, Miss Lily; I'll look after the little maid while all this is going on.' I felt

embarrassed, but she nodded at me and said almost under her breath, 'Take a few minutes off, lover. 'twill do you good after all that unhappiness last night.'

I knew then that she understood, and I needed to have no fears about Mary for the next half hour. So I left the kitchen and ran up to my room to find a shawl, and to pin on my hat more securely, for I knew being out on the water it would be wild and blowy.

Matt was waiting by his boat on the river beach when I got there, and gave me a hand as I climbed aboard. 'Like old times, maid,' he said, and his smile told me how glad he was that we were together again. But even so, something uncomfortable in my mind said, *This can't last. Things are different now. You belong with the Frobishers, not with Matt.*

But then the motion of the boat as he took the oars and rowed us out of the harbour, through the strong currents of the estuary and then into the sea, where

the waves rolled and sang, reminded me of all the childish enjoyment I had had with him, and I found myself puzzled and confused about what I was doing.

I dangled my hand over the side of the boat and felt the surge and power of the ocean, and then forgot everything except Matt and the way he rowed over to the buoy which signaled the position of his crab pots. And then I was helping him to pull up the ropes and empty the crabs into the basket at the stern of the boat, laughing with him as he shouted, against the noise of the gulls following us and the pounding of the sea, 'I'll give you a crab to take back to your master, Lily. Then he'll forgive you for running off and going to sea with a fisherman. Maybe he'll even let you do it again!'

By the time he had rowed back into the harbour, beached the boat and found a little basket in which to put one of the live crabs, I felt exhilarated. The wind and the roar of the sea had done me good, and being with Matt had

been a brief moment of great enjoyment which I told myself I would not forget, even though my position as Mary's nursemaid meant we were bound to drift apart. I walked up the beach with new confidence in myself, knowing that even if the past held unhappy memories, the way I lived now was making new and much happier ones.

8

I went into the house by the back door and showed Mary and Mrs Hodge the crab in my small basket. Mary wanted to pick it up, and found her finger being nipped; she backed away, tears in her eyes, and Mrs Hodge said, 'Never mind, maid, you'll get your own back on the little chap when I put his claw on your plate tomorrow luncheon. Now, off upstairs with Miss Lily, take these shells with you, and be sure to wash your hands clean before you come down to see your papa later on this afternoon.'

She looked across the room at me, and I saw her kind eyes were warm and concerned. 'Feeling better, Miss Lily, are you, now? I guess that wherever you've been has done you good — you look bright and happy again. You know what they say — all work and no play

don't do no one any good.'

I smiled and felt my cheeks redden, but nodded. 'Yes, Mrs Hodge, and thank you for looking after Mary.'

She turned back to the pan bubbling on the oven behind her, but looked over her shoulder. 'Any time, my dear, I'll always look after the little maid. And perhaps you should ask Mr Daniel for more time off — he'll understand, I'm sure, nice man that he is.'

And so the days passed, quiet and happy as Mary and I discovered parts of Teignmouth we hadn't visited for a long time, like the Wintergarden where concerts were held, and even took the ferry over to Shaldon. Mary was excited by this, and I had a job making her sit still while the ferryman rowed across the river.

'When can I get out?' she asked impatiently.

I laughed as I said, 'When we ground on the other side! Don't want to get your feet wet, do you?' And she made a face.

'But I'd like to paddle. Can I take off my shoes and stockings when we land on the beach?'

I didn't answer at once, for this was a tricky question. I knew that once Mary had felt the sand and water between her toes she would want to do it every day, and I didn't think this was a good idea. Yes, she wasn't quite as wild as she had been when I first took charge of her, but still her eyes lit up at the thought of any excitement. So although I allowed her to have a short paddle once we were safely on Shaldon beach, I soon dried her off, put her shoes and stockings on again, and took her for a walk to look in the chandler's window where things like anchors and sailors' hats and boots and ropes were, apparently, very exciting indeed to a small girl who lived in a quiet house with a quiet papa and a restraining nursemaid!

That night, as she got into bed waiting for her story, I concocted a tale about Becky falling off her father's fishing boat and having to swim to the

shore. And then telling everyone she would never, NEVER, go near the water again! And I hoped Mary would take all this in, and behave accordingly.

But as she closed her eyes and snuggled down into her bed, she had a last question. 'How long is never, Lily? Does it go on and on?'

'Yes,' I said firmly, 'it goes on forever. Now, off to sleep, Mary, and sweet dreams.' And by the time I reached the door and looked back, she was asleep. I hoped very much that the last few words would stay with her.

Later that evening, as I was preparing for bed, Mrs Hodge knocked at my door. When I opened it I thought she looked as if she had something good to tell me. 'Come in, Mrs Hodge,' I said. 'Take the chair, and I'll sit on the bed.'

* * *

She grinned at me. 'Well, lover, a bit of news to cheer you up. Your young man, Matt Boyne — isn't that him, owns the

boat *Daisy Lee?*'

I nodded, wondering what Matt wanted now.

Clearly, Mrs Hodge was longing to tell me. 'He came to the door this afternoon and said could he leave a message for you.' Her red face broadened even further as the smile grew. 'Of course, I said yes — told him I wouldn't be able to deliver it till dinner was over — and well, here I am now, to tell you.'

Inside me, something awkward twisted as I thought of being with Matt. I knew I had enjoyed his company, accompanying him to fetch in his crab pots; but coming here, and leaving a message? Whatever could he want to say?

Very carefully, I said, 'Good of you to tell me all this, Mrs Hodge, and I'm sorry you had the bother. But what can he want to say to me?'

She raised her hands as if in pleasure, and her voice was warm. 'Why, that he wants to see you, maid! He said be on

the beach tomorrow morning early before he goes out with the tide, and then you and he can arrange something!'

I was shocked. Matt knew that my position as Mary's nursemaid meant that I had charge of her from the moment she awoke to her last hug at night. How could he possibly expect me to slip out after breakfast and leave her? And that brought back memories of playing with Matt as a young child — he always was the one to make the plans, to lead and make me follow. Was he doing the same thing now? And if so — I felt anger kindle inside me and got up from the bed, pacing around the small room — he must learn that life was different now, so very different. No longer could I do whatever he wanted, and somehow I must tell him that. But we had been so happy as children playing together, and the last thing I wanted was to hurt him.

I sank down on the bed again and looked into Mrs Hodge's mystified

face. 'I'm sorry,' I said, 'but there's no way I can meet Matt in the morning. And he shouldn't expect me to. So he'll be cross, of course, when I'm not there, but . . . '

We looked at each other for a few moments, and then she said, 'But I thought he were your young man; that you cared for him. And I could always look after Miss Mary for a short time, you know.'

She searched my face with her faded eyes, looking quite sad, and so I said, 'Thank you, Mrs Hodge, but I shan't be going to see him. I'll . . . well, I expect we'll met on the beach in a day or so, and then I'll tell him.'

She interrupted me sharply. 'That he's not your young man, is that it?'

I nodded. 'That's right, Mrs Hodge. I could never love Matt Boyne — not now, now that my life has taken a different direction, you see.'

Another long pause, until stiffly she got to her feet, pushed the chair back against the wall and went towards the

door. Then she turned back, looking at me, pulling her wrapper more closely around her as she said quietly, 'Well, as long as you know your own mind, Miss Lily, I suppose that's all that matters. And if the young man calls again I'll tell him you're out, or busy, shall I?'

'I-I don't know . . . ' But I did, of course. Matt would never give up so easily. And sometime soon I must meet him and tell him the truth. It would be difficult, and at the moment I refused to think about it. I was tired. I needed my sleep. So I said, with the warmest smile I could force onto my face, 'Thank you, Mrs Hodge. And now perhaps we should forget all about Matt, and settle down for the night. It's getting late, and I think we both need our beauty sleep, don't we?'

That made her laugh, and she was still laughing as she left the room and headed for her own, just down the passage, her last words echoing as she went: 'That's something I need a lot more of than you do, my lover. Well,

goodnight, and sleep well.'

As I slipped into bed I heard her door shut, and told myself I must stop thinking about Matt. But it was difficult, and I lay there for a long time, wondering just what I should tell him when the moment came.

★ ★ ★

Next day I was still wondering, but life with Mary kept me busy, and I was happy enough as we passed the morning colouring in her flower book and checking with the reference book to make sure we knew the names of all the pretty blooms she was looking at.

'Look, Lily — here's a lily!' Her eyes widened and she stared down at the page. 'It doesn't look like you, does it?' Which made us both laugh, and clearly it was still in her mind when, after luncheon with Mr Daniel, she slipped out of her chair and went to his side, whispering to him and looking at me over her shoulder with a big smile. I

smiled back, and left her there, thinking it was nice for her to have a few moments privately with her papa, who was always so busy with the emporium, and having little time to spend at home with his daughter.

I went up to the nursery to tidy up before we dressed ready for our afternoon walk, and started wondering when Mrs Frobisher would return home. As I pinned on my hat, I saw my reflection in the mirror and knew I was looking worried. For I had a feeling that the nice and easy relationship I had at the moment with Mr Daniel would somehow, and for some reason, be bound to change. And then, standing quite still, pulling on my gloves, I faced a truth which suddenly confronted me, and knew that I should be very sad when that happened. For Mr Daniel was always kind to me, always finding a smile, even when in a hurry, and finding little fault with my care of his wayward daughter. Even when Mary had told him about paddling on the

Shaldon beach, he had simply glanced at me, and almost grinned, saying very quietly, 'I'm glad you pulled her out in time, Miss Lily. And that there was no need to call the lifeboat.'

I had replied with a quick grin of my own, saying very quietly, 'Please don't get her thinking about the lifeboat, Mr Daniel, or else she'll be wanting to go and listen out for the maroons, and then I'll never get her home again!' We had both laughed, and then Mary had stopped whispering and had taken his hand, pulling him with her, going to the window to look out at the racing sea, and I had left the room.

That afternoon we walked to the Seaspray Café to have some lemonade and a newly baked biscuit so that Mary could play with Bobby. Jess was laying tables and there were no other customers, so she sat down for a few minutes to talk to me. 'I heard that you went out with Matt Boyne the other day, Lily — old Jake Roper saw you helping with the crab pots, and of course it was all

round the town in a few minutes. Seeing him again, are you? I know you were fond of each other as children.' Her smile broadened and her eyes gleamed. 'Getting serious, are you, now? Do tell!'

Alarm suddenly filled me. If rumours were abounding, what would happen if they reached the emporium and the ears of Mr Daniel? What if he thought I was likely to leave Mary in order to marry Matt? And I could only thank goodness that Mrs Frobisher was away, for surely in her old-fashioned ways, she would have ordered her staff to have no followers, and to hear of me going crabbing with a fisherman would have finished my career as a nursemaid.

I stared at Jess and her smile faded. 'What's wrong? What have I said?'

I leaned across the table. 'Too much, Jess, much too much. I don't want people talking about me.'

She came back sharply. 'Then you shouldn't have gone out with him, should you? Don't blame me, Lily, for if

people talk about you then it's your own fault.' She smiled again. 'Here, have another biscuit and cheer up. I can't imagine that Mr Daniel would want to find fault with you for doing something so natural. Just an hour in a boat! Couldn't get up to any mischief there, could you?' And her smile was that saucy grin again, which did cheer me a little.

But as Mary and I retraced our steps homeward, I learned a little bit more about myself and my feelings. I would see Matt and tell him we had no future together, and I would attend better to my duties, for I knew I owed Mr Daniel a great deal. He was a nice man, and I didn't want to add to any worries he must have running his emporium. In fact, it dawned on me with a considerable jolt that I liked Mr Daniel — a lot.

That evening, Mary was grinning and looking at me as if she had a secret which she half-wanted to share but couldn't quite bring herself to do so. I wondered, slightly alarmed, if she was

planning something really mischievous, so got down the book Mr Daniel had given her for her last birthday, which was *The Wind in the Willows*, and together we read about the adventures of Mole and Ratty and that awful Mr Toad. Mary, of course, saw him as the hero, and so we had a lot of 'tooting' and playing at being in motor cars as we tidied up and got ready to go down and see Mr Daniel prior to having dinner together.

As we descended the stairs, Mary wearing a new dress Mrs Frobisher had sent from London, and looking a picture in the bright green velvet which brought out the innocent brightness of her eyes, I wished secretly that I had something new to wear. A lovely dress which would perhaps make Mr Daniel look at me in a new way.

9

Mr Daniel duly admired Mary in her new dress, and then looked across at me. 'Just the thing for when she goes to the dance competition, surely, Lily?'

I was amazed. Mary's wish to be part of the competition on the pier had been at the back of my mind for a few days, but no idea had come as to how I could divert her. Yet here was her papa suggesting she should go. My face must have shown my surprise as I said carefully, 'I didn't think you would approve of her entering the competition, Mr Daniel.'

He waited a few seconds as if making up his mind, then said, 'Mr Browning, the pier manager, came to see me yesterday and suggested I should allow Mary — with you, of course, looking after her — to enter. There is to be a children's class which would be quite

suitable, and Dulcie Rowan, who runs the dance school in the town, is to be the judge.' A smile slowly spread over his face and he put his hand on Mary's arm, standing beside his chair. 'I thought it might be good for Mary to understand she isn't the only important one, but just a small girl in the company of several others, some of whom will have more talent than she has. But if you are against it, Lily, then I understand.' He looked at me enquiringly.

I thought hard. Yes, it was a very good idea to bring down Mary's already overrated opinion of herself, and how sensible of him to think like that. So I could only nod and say, 'No, Mr Daniel, I'm not against it. In fact I think it would be very good. And I will most certainly take her on Friday afternoon — it starts at half past five, I believe.'

His smile told me I had pleased him. 'Very well, then, and perhaps I can find ten minutes to come and watch the

performance.' He put an arm around his daughter, looking at him with her wide blue eyes. 'Yes, my love, you shall dance, and you will also learn, along with the dance steps and the rhythm of the music, that you're not the only little girl in the world. And so I think it will be an important day for you.'

Of course Mary didn't realise quite what he was telling her. I could see that she was only thinking of wearing the new dress and dancing around the café on the pier with everybody smiling and clapping her. But a new warmth spread through me as I realised that Mr Daniel cared very much for his spoiled little girl, and was doing what he thought right to help her mend her ways. And as her nursemaid, I would certainly do all I could to help.

I took Mary up to the nursery at bedtime and told her to hang up her new dress herself instead of just letting it lie on the floor when she took it off. She looked at me with a frown. 'But you always do it, Lily!'

Without really thinking, I said, 'I may not always be here, Mary, so I think you should learn to look after yourself in some ways. Please pick it up; here's the hanger, and you can find a place in the wardrobe among your other clothes.'

Slowly she did so, and then came back to me, looking at me without the usual lovely smile, her eyes wider than ever. 'But I want you to be here always, Lily. Please don't go away.' And she clung to me, her small arms warm around my body.

I shouldn't have said that. But, excusing myself, I knew that for her own good she must learn about life. Mr Daniel and I both thought so. So I soothed her, stroked her hair, and held her close, saying gently, 'I don't want to go away, Mary, and I never want to leave you. Now, cheer up, and think about the dance competition . . . ' As she did so, quickly smiling again, I realised that what I had said was because the dark memory of my mother — Dodie — leaving me still stayed in

my mind. I was determined that Mary must never go through that.

Friday became all important then, with Mary practising her twists and twirls wherever she could find a space, and me hanging on to her hand before she could quite escape. We went to see Jess again so that Mary could show Bobby just how good she was at dancing, and try to teach him some steps. Jess and I chatted when she had a moment from serving teas and coffees, and I told her about Matt sending me a message.

She frowned at me. 'So what are you going to do? You can't just ignore him, poor boy. He must be very fond of you, Lily. Couldn't you somehow take an hour off and go out with him? And then you could explain how you feel.'

I rescued Mary from a particularly tough step Bobby had decided to teach her, and said quickly, 'But I don't know how I feel. Not really. I need time to think it over.'

Jess carried her tray of empty cups

towards the kitchen and said sharply over her shoulder, 'Then get on with it. So unkind to keep him waiting. And now I think you must go, before Mary makes Bobby even more cross. Goodbye, Lily, till next time.' And she disappeared, pulling the door to behind her.

I collected Mary, tidied her unbuttoned coat, and turned her hat the right way around. We left the café, heading the opposite way from the road towards the river beach. I knew I was in the wrong frame of mind to see Matt now. It was a problem that I pushed to the back of my mind, but, try as I would, it never really went away. I told myself, *Yes, all right, I will find him and tell him how I feel, but not at the moment.*

And then it was Thursday, and Mary was so excited about the dance competition the next day that it was hard to know what to do to keep her quiet. But at breakfast Mr Daniel looked across the table at me and said, 'I think I will take Mary to the

emporium for a while this morning; she can be amused in the toy department where the sales girls will look after her, and you can have a little time to yourself.'

I must have looked surprised, for he added, 'I know Mary takes a lot of looking after, Lily, and I don't want you to be too tired. So enjoy yourself this morning — and I'll bring Mary home for luncheon.' He smiled. 'Perhaps a stroll on the beach? Or even a meeting with some of your friends? You know what they say about all work and no play . . . '

His smile became a laugh and I joined in, saying without really thinking, 'Why, that's what my Aunt Edie said!' And then I bit my lip, because at once I thought of Dodie — my mother — and my aunt, and wondered if they had resolved their differences.

Again, my telltale expression must have touched him, for he leaned towards me and said very quietly, away from Mary's hearing, 'I hope being

here, Lily, hasn't caused any problems with your family? If so, you must let me know, and perhaps I can do something to help, like giving you more time off.'

I felt a lump come in my throat and I said, 'Thank you, Mr Daniel.' The words were ready to rush out and tell him about my mother coming back into my life and how difficult it all was, but somehow I kept them unsaid. He was such a nice, helpful man that I knew I mustn't bother him with more problems, for surely running the big emporium produced enough without my adding any more. So I swallowed the lump and said a bit unsteadily, 'That's very considerate of you, Mr Daniel, and I appreciate your kindness.'

His dark eyes softened as he looked at me then. 'It's easy to be kind to you, Lily — you're a good, hard-working girl and, in my turn, I appreciate all you do for my family. If ever I can help with anything, don't be afraid to tell me, will you?'

I met his gaze, feeling my emotions

rise, for he was showing me such an unexpected part of himself that I felt much nearer to him than before. So kind. So thoughtful. So full of warmth . . .

And then Mary, tired of not being noticed, slipped down from her chair and started dancing round the room. 'Tomorrow,' she sang at the top of her high little voice. 'Tomorrow we'll all be dancing!' Beside my chair she stopped and grabbed my hands. 'Come on, Lily, time to start dancing!'

Mr Daniel got up, picked her up and moved her away from me. 'Now, young lady,' he said, smiling down at her. 'You're giving Lily a bit of a holiday, and you can spend the morning looking at all the new toys in the emporium. Run upstairs and get your coat and hat, and we'll be off. We'll walk along the seafront, and you can tell me everything you hope for tomorrow at the dance competition. Hurry up — we mustn't keep customers waiting for us to open the shop, you know.'

I got up, feeling a little awkward, and watched them go into the hall, where Mary scampered upstairs while Mr Daniel waited patiently for her. And then they were off, father and daughter, clearly happy to be together, walking briskly along the seafront, looking at each other and talking. I waited until they were out of sight and then went up to the nursery, where I tidied things up, made my bed, and then put on my coat. I wasn't sure where I would spend this special time given to me, but I discovered my feet walking towards Regent Row, and before I knew it I was in the bakery, looking at a surprised Aunt Edie who was pummeling dough on the big table while Dodie — Mother — stood by the fire, watching. And by the tone of their voices, although I didn't at once hear the words, I knew problems were in the air. But slowly it became clear: Aunt Edie was still unforgiving about her sister having abandoned me with her.

'But at least you could have written,

not just disappeared without a word for all those years. The maid's nineteen now, and that's a long time without her mother. I can't forgive you, Dodie, so don't go on about it any longer. I've got this bread to make, and a business to run on my own, so just go away and leave me in peace.' Aunt Edie slammed down the dough until I thought it must break into small lumps.

Standing just inside the door, I saw the expression on my mother's face slowly become contorted and realised tears were ready to fall. So instinctively I ran to her side and put an arm around her shoulders. 'Don't cry, Mother. I'm sure Aunt Edie is only letting free all her thoughts from the past. She'll come round in the end.'

As she opened the door and stepped outside, she glanced back at me and I saw how hurt and sad she was. But she wiped her eyes and took a deep breath. 'Edie was always obstinate, but I shall keep on trying. You see, I want to get my life back together with my family.

Well, I've found you, dearest Lily, and now I must do all I can to persuade Edie that we can be fond sisters once more if she'll let me. I shan't give in.' And then, smiling sadly, she reached up and kissed my cheek. And before I could reply, or return the embrace, she turned and quickly walked away, the empty flower baskets caught up in both hands.

I stayed where I was in the doorway, watching her until she turned the corner and was gone. And then I went back into the shop and looked at Aunt Edie, who stood at the table red-faced, wisps of grey hair falling out of her cap, looking tired as she pushed loaves into the huge oven that heated the whole bakery. I realised for perhaps the first time in my life just how hard she worked. The bakery was hers and she worked alone in it, although I knew by now that she had engaged a young girl to help out in the mornings and who I saw now, coming in from the back room with a broom and sweeping up

the fallen flour, just as I had done when I worked here. Something in me — a hard knot of some sort — untied then, and I felt much happier.

Walking slowly back to the Esplanade, enjoying the sun, hearing the gulls and the music of the waves as they rolled up the golden beach, I knew I was learning many lessons. Some were about Aunt Edie and her hard work; some about young Mary, who also needed to learn lessons; and most of all about my mother who, despite living such a hard life, had enough warmth and determination in her to return and try and regain her family's love.

And then, as I entered the house, walking through the kitchen and smiling at Mrs Hodge, I realised that the most important lessons I was learning were about myself. And I also knew that somewhere in there, among the list of new thoughts, Mr Daniel stood, strong and helpful and with something in his eyes that, as I remembered, began to excite me.

I went up to the nursery and tidied away some of Mary's clothes and toys, and although I worked efficiently, my mind was full of that new, warmer expression on his face, and in his dark eyes, when he had smiled at me that morning.

10

On Friday I took Mary for a walk along the sea wall beside the railway line, mostly to quieten her and also to ensure that she would be ready for a rest in the afternoon, before the dance competition. Beside me, she screamed wildly and put her hands to her ears as the trains rushed past us, and then asked if we could go for a train ride one day.

I said carefully, 'I expect so, Mary, but I must ask your papa if he thinks we should do so. Trains are rattly and noisy and perhaps you might not like riding in one. But we'll see.'

Quiet again, walking beside me, she looked up with that big smile and said, 'I expect Bobby would like to be in a train, but what I would really like to do, Lily, is to go to the flower lady's garden again and see her lovely flowers

growing. Can we go, please?'

It was easy to reply, for as she spoke my memory took me back to sitting at the tea table with Dorothy — Mother — while Mary paddled in the stream, and I found myself agreeing with her. Yes, it would be lovely to return. So I said, 'Yes, we will. We'll ask your papa if Eddie can drive us there one afternoon next week.'

'But next week is your birthday, Lily! And we have to go to see Mrs Drew and collect your cake on Tuesday.' She tugged at my hand and broke into a skip. 'Isn't it all exciting? And the dance competition after tea . . . ' Her laughter rang out in the fresh salt air, and I felt a warm glow spread over me. Mary was happy, and I should be, too. So many ideas were awaiting us as the days passed, how could I possibly let family problems and thoughts of Matt bear me down?

* * *

In the afternoon I persuaded Mary to rest, and was glad to see her eyes shut as I read a few pages of our favourite book to her. I knew that the dance competition would bring great excitement, and it was a good thing that she could be quiet for a short while before getting dressed up and telling me, over and over, as she had this morning, that she was going to dance very well and make people clap and smile.

After tea I took her along the seafront to the pier, where crowds of local people were waiting to be admitted. The man at the entrance recognized us — I supposed he knew Mr Daniel would be coming — and so we walked the length of the pier to the café, where the manager greeted us and showed us to our seats in the front row of the chairs lined up for the audience. Mary found it hard to sit still, but I managed to take off her hat and coat and put them on my lap, while she fidgeted on her chair.

'Is it time for me to dance, Lily?'

'Not yet, Mary. We have to wait for the lady playing the piano to come, and also Miss Rowan, the dance lady, to appear. She will watch you all dancing, you see, and then give out marks as to who has done the best.' I wanted to warn Mary that other small children could well dance better than she did, but it was hard to get into her overexcited mind.

'What marks?' she asked, looking puzzled.

'Well, you could get five out of ten if you dance moderately well, or perhaps eight or nine if you do better than that. It's just a way of judging the competition.'

'I shall get nine!' she said determinedly. 'Or even ten . . . '

'Don't be too sure, Mary. Other children may be more experienced at dancing, and so leave you with a lower mark.' I tried hard to damp down that pride, and saw her face fall for a moment.

And then things were happening. The

pianist sat down and started playing, and Miss Rowan appeared with the pier manager beside her, and was given a chair in the middle of the room. But at first she didn't sit down; she came to the front of the little stage, where the curtains had been drawn open, and smiled at us all.

'Another dance competition is here,' she said in a warm, rich voice. 'And another lot of up-and-coming dancers to entertain us. But to start with, and to get into the mood for dancing, I want all the little entrants to come up here and show us how they can dance together.' She turned towards the pianist. 'May we have 'Ring a Ring o' Roses', please? And children, come up here onto the stage and form a nice circle, will you?'

I whispered to Mary, 'Do as she says, and join the others up there, Mary — and dance as well as you can.'

It was a delight to watch how the other children — seven of them altogether, including two small boys

— joined hands and then, slowly at first, and then more quickly as their nervousness died, danced around to the famous old tune the pianist was playing. And of course they all fell down at the end, smiles and giggles having the audience laughing and clapping. When they were on their feet again, Miss Rowan congratulated them all on their concentration and their easy movement, and then called out the first dancer to perform while the others disappeared into the wings to watch.

Little Charlotte Webb, the fishmonger's youngest daughter, looked very timid; but as the music filled the room she forgot her shyness and began to drift around the stage, arms out and elegantly floating in the air, legs rhythmically moving to the beat of the piano. She eventually smiled as she ended her little performance, coming to the front and curtseying, and all without falling down. Applause soared around us and the little girl went off into the wings looking amazed and

pleased with herself.

A few minutes later Miss Rowan called, 'The next dancer, please.' And so it went on.

Mr Daniel came quite soon, seating himself beside me and whispering, 'She hasn't danced yet, I hope, Lily?'

I answered, 'Not yet. But at any moment, I think.'

We sat there entranced by the little dancers, each of whom had their own few steps to perform, and when Mary's turn came around I felt Mr Daniel sit up a bit straighter beside me. I glanced at him, and we both smiled. 'Now we shall see,' he whispered, and inside me I glowed. He was sharing his love of his daughter with me, and that meant so much. Instantly I forgot the rows between my mother and Aunt Edie, and the fact that soon I must seek out Matt and explain the situation to him. All that mattered was that Mary's papa and I were here together, sharing a very important moment in his daughter's life.

Mary danced beautifully. She had lost her initial nervousness, and now she skipped into the centre of the stage and curtsied to Miss Rowan, which led to a moment of applause. Her smile grew and then she lost herself in the numerous steps she had practised so keenly, and tried to teach Bobby, and which resulted in a small but elegant dance movement. Her arms floated, her little body swayed with lovely balance, and her small feet pointed and lifted in time to the music. When she had finished, standing neatly and looking down at Miss Rowan, there was more applause, and Mr Daniel turned to me, his smile very broad. He put his hand on mine, clasped in my lap.

'Perhaps not a Petrova — not yet — but a beautiful little performance. Did you enjoy it as I did, Lily?'

I felt the warmth of his slender, strong fingers, and my voice trembled as I whispered back, 'I did, oh yes, I did, Mr Daniel. You must be so proud of her.'

He nodded and removed his hand, but kept looking at me. 'And you're the one who must be thanked for helping with all that practice, Lily, and I shan't forget all your care and help. And now you must take the young ballerina home and I must return to the emporium, as I have a meeting to attend. But I shall see you both before bedtime — and I look forward to doing so. Goodbye.' He stood up, waved to Mary who was making her way towards us, and then left the café.

Mary ran to my side, her face dimmed of the usual smile. 'Where is Papa? He's gone back to the emporium, hasn't he? Oh, but I wanted to be with him, to know what marks I've got, and what he thought of my dancing . . . Oh, it's not fair.'

Her eyes swam and quickly I helped her on with coat and hat and said, 'Sit down for a few more minutes, Mary, while we hear the marks. And you will talk to your papa about the dancing this

evening, so no more tears, if you please.'

Miss Rowan was on her feet amid claps and began reading out the marks. Suddenly all was very silent. 'Master Albert Dunstone, winner of the competition, nine marks, on account of his clever little jumps and the splendid movement of his hands.'

Mary, beside me, looked discouraged and muttered, 'I could have done some jumps — I didn't know you could.'

I didn't answer, because the list of marks was continuing. And then, 'Mary Frobisher, who danced with such elegance and pleasure, eight marks. Well done, Mary, and I would like you to continue with your dancing, please.' Miss Rowan looked around the room, found us, and smiled encouragingly.

At once Mary was her usual smiling self again. She did a little jig as she stood by the chair, and looked first at Miss Rowan, and then back at me. 'Eight marks is good, isn't it, Lily?'

'It is excellent, Mary — how well you

have done. And not winning the competition doesn't matter, for you heard what Miss Rowan said — that you must continue practising your dancing, which means you will improve and get better and better. But now we must go home. Come along.'

We left the pier and walked back along the Esplanade. We were within sight of home when the figure of Matt appeared, saw us, and then waited until we reached his side. My breath was tight, and I was unsure what I was going to say, but he quickly got in first.

'At last! I've been waiting for you to come and find me, Lily. You got my message, didn't you? But you weren't there next morning.'

His voice, usually so warm and gentle, held a harsh note, and I wondered how to reply, with Mary listening to every word. But eventually I said slowly, 'I'm sorry, Matt, but it isn't possible for me to meet you like that. I told you last time that things are different now.' I stopped and felt my

hands tighten, still holding Mary's. But it was necessary to make him understand. My voice trembled as I went on, 'You see, I'm employed by the Frobisher family, and so — '

Here he cut in, his expression darkening with every word. 'And so you don't want a fisherman friend any more, is that it? Well, Lily, I shan't give up, and I'll expect you to change your mind and then come and find me. Understand?' He stepped nearer, put his hand to my face and cupped it, adding more gently, 'I want to kiss you, Lily, but not with the little miss watching. Next time . . . ' He turned quickly and strode away down the road, with Mary and me still standing there, her hand in mine so tightly clenched.

I forced myself to return to reality and let go of her hand, saying in as controlled a voice as I could manage, 'Oh dear, Matt was in a really bad temper, wasn't he? But never mind. We'll go home and talk about the

dancing. Come along, Mary, we're nearly there.'

Thank goodness for the peace and quietness of the nursery, the warmth of the small fire, and the business of hanging up Mary's best dress and listening to her chattering on about how Charlotte and Albert danced, and what she intended to do in the future about her dancing. 'Grandmother will be pleased, won't she? 'specially as I was wearing that pretty dress she gave me.' The clock on the mantelpiece struck seven and she ran to the door. 'It's time to go down and see Papa now, Lily. Come on.'

Away she went, downstairs and into the drawing room, with me following more sedately, and hoping that the unpleasant scene with Matt had already left her busy little mind. But as soon as we entered the room, to find Mr Daniel sorting out some papers on the table by the window, she ran over to him and said, 'Poor Lily. We met her friend Matt, and he was horrible to her. But

let's talk about the dancing, Papa.'

He sat down — wearily, I thought — in his mother's armchair, and Mary perched on his knee, looking at him with a huge smile and wide eyes. 'Did you think I danced well? Miss Rowan did.'

At once Mr Daniel's expression cleared as he looked at her overjoyed face. He said quietly, 'I thought you were wonderful, my love.' But then, as she chattered on about practising every day and perhaps even doing jumps like Albert did, he looked at me, and his expression altered.

I knew him well enough now to know that he wouldn't let Mary's thoughtless words go unchallenged, and I was at a loss to know just what to say. So, when all the chatter about dancing was over and he turned and looked at me very seriously, I flushed. If he asked about Matt, what on earth could I say? That I was turning down a very old friend, because my feelings were now elsewhere?

11

That evening as Mary and I left the drawing room, having discussed the competition and Mary's excellent performance, Mr Daniel said quietly to me, 'Lily, please come down when Mary is asleep. I should like to talk to you — I feel her future needs discussing, and I know that you will have some sensible ideas to add to mine.'

I was uplifted, and went to the nursery smiling. What a good, kind employer he was. And then other words ran through my head — what a strong, warm and thoughtful man he was. I was so fortunate to be here in his house, part of his family. I just hoped it would continue like this for a long time yet. But then, as Mary snuggled into her bed and closed her eyes — and she must be tired, after all that excitement,

I thought — something else came to mind. Mary's future, he had said. But Mary would soon be more of a young lady than a small child. Would she still need a nursemaid? Was that part of the discussion he had suggested we might have? What ideas might he have already planned?

I went downstairs slowly, suddenly feeling a shadow in my life. What would I do when Mary no longer needed me? I must have shown those unhappy thoughts on my face as I entered the drawing room, where Mr Daniel stood by the fireplace, coming over to me at once and gesturing to his mother's armchair.

'Sit down, Lily. I hope you're warm? Comfortable? Good. And so to our talk. Yes, I think we must make plans about Mary, who is growing up so fast. She may be just a six and a half years old at the moment, but time flies, as I'm sure you'll agree. And at the back of my mind is what my mother said to me before she went up to London — that

Mary's education must not be delayed much longer.'

I sat there, feeling stiff and suddenly chilled. So this was it. Mary must be educated, and clearly her nursemaid must find other employment. After a short pause, while his eyes were on my face, I managed a smile and said, 'Of course I agree, Mr Daniel. She is an intelligent child, and will soon be ready for more instruction than I am qualified to give. At the moment we read together, and she manages very well, even quite long words. But as to other subjects . . . '

'Other subjects are not what I'm thinking about particularly, Lily.' His voice was firm as he settled himself in a chair opposite mine. 'What I'm concerned about is her social life. She needs interaction with other children, because I see her already growing vain and overconfident. And I can't allow my only daughter to grow up in such a way.' He leaned forward in his chair and his smile cheered me a little. 'But, Lily,

please don't think I'm saying all this because I aim to get rid of your services. Indeed, no — for what would Mary do without you? Your warm heart and understanding have helped her to recover from the death of her mother, and I'm grateful for all you have done; so thankful for your ability to help her to think of brighter things and to live a happier life.'

Inside me that knot which had been growing tighter and tighter slowly untied itself, and I relaxed into the comfort of the armchair. I couldn't speak for a moment as I realised what he was saying, and then understood that I could still live here with him and Mary for more time than I had realised at first.

I found it difficult to find the right words, and all I could manage was, 'Thank you, Mr Daniel. And of course I'm only too pleased to do all I can for Mary — and you — for as long as you continue to need me.'

They must have been the right

words, for he sat back then, stretching his legs in front of him, and smiling more expansively at me. 'Thank you, Lily. But I want you to think it over, and if later you feel it would be better for your career — or your own personal life — to leave now, rather than later, I shall understand. But if that does happen, I can only say that Mary won't be the only one to miss you, for I shall, also. You see . . . ' He stopped and I watched how his face slowly eased, the tense lines fading. 'I have been lonely, Lily, since my wife died. Grief is a painful business, and having you here with Mary, removing the anxiety about her, has certainly helped me to get on with my life.'

We sat in silence then, he bending to put a few pieces of coal on the flickering fire, and me thinking that I felt happier than I had thought possible. The atmosphere, I sensed, was growing relaxed and free. Mr Daniel was suddenly no longer my employer but my friend. So, when he smiled

.cross the space separating us and asked quietly, 'Would you like to tell me about your home life, Lily?', it seemed just a casual question which I was ready to answer without fear or embarrassment.

'When I was about two years old my mother left me with my aunt,' I said, and saw how he frowned, as if he cared. 'My Aunt Edie, who runs the bakery.' I smiled. 'Where Mary and I will go on Tuesday to collect the cake she is making for my birthday.'

'Which is on Wednesday.' The frown disappeared.

'Yes, it is. I suppose Mary has told you?'

'She has, several times.' He was more lighthearted than I had ever known him to be, I thought — even amused. 'And I shall be at home on Wednesday afternoon, all ready for the party.'

'The party? Oh, goodness, Mr Daniel . . . '

'But of course you must have a party. Mary will never forgive me if it's just

tea by the fire with a bit of rich cake. I think we should go out into the country, perhaps have a picnic. What do you think of that?'

At once I knew just what I was thinking. Quickly I said, 'Mary wants to go and see the flower lady's garden again. Could we, perhaps . . . ?'

'Never mind what Mary wants. Would you like that, Lily?'

The words came out clear and free. 'I should love it, Mr Daniel. You see, the flower lady — Dorothy Ross — is my mother.' I heard my voice lighten. 'She has come back looking for me, and although I wasn't happy at first, now I'm beginning to accept her as my mother, and so . . . ' I stopped and felt my face going pink, for surely I had said too much. He couldn't possibly want to know all this. I sat back in my chair and clasped my hands tightly in front of me, adding unevenly and not looking at his keen, dark eyes, 'But you don't want to hear about that. I'm sorry, Mr Daniel. Please forgive me.'

Although I looked at the carpet in front of my chair, I was aware of him getting up, crossing to stand near me, then leaning down and taking my cold hands in his, carefully drawing me to my feet. He stood for a long, silent moment, and then slowly he let go of my hands and raised his own to cup my face, so that I could do nothing but meet his eyes. 'Lily, you don't understand, do you? I'm interested in anything you care to tell me. You've helped me to recover my interest in life, and now, you see . . . ' His voice dropped, the next words almost a whisper. 'My interest in you is growing fast.'

What could I say? I felt my heart start to race. Daniel stood so near me — suddenly I knew I could drop the title of 'mister' — that a feeling of longing spread through my entire body. He was so tall, so handsome, so . . . Words eluded me and then, because of my strict upbringing, shame replaced the longing. What was I doing? This

149

man was my employer, my insurance against a poor and lonely old age. I must respect him and keep my place as a mere nursemaid. I stepped away, half-stumbling over the chair behind me, and at once he saved me, drawing me away from danger and smiling as he said, 'Lily, don't be afraid. I just want you to know that Mary and I have both grown fond of you. And I hope that makes you happy.'

What could I say? Instinct took over; I must accept all that he said, and not let him know how I felt just now. A nursemaid falling for her employer! Ridiculous and wicked. He must never know.

'Of course it does, Mr Daniel. I can think of you now — ' A lump in my throat, quickly swallowed. ' — as a real friend. I hope that will be all right?'

Did I detect an expression of dismay sliding over his face? Of course not. So I added, lightly and with what I hoped was amusement in my voice, 'A girl like me usually has only local friends — Jess

in the café, and Matt with his trawler
. . . So to have you also as a friend will
be wonderful.'

I stopped abruptly, unable to look at
his face any longer. I turned away,
ready to go back to the nursery, but he
stopped me, saying, 'Why yes — so
Matt is the friend who Mary told me
was being hateful to you?'

At the doorway I turned and said
slowly, and unwillingly, 'Yes, he is. We
were once very good friends — in our
childhood. And he wants us to carry
on, but, but . . . He thinks that now I
work for you I'm growing indifferent to
him. He was very hurt, and I apologise
for letting Mary hear what he said.'

'Mary must grow used to hearing
words which are full of other things
than mere enjoyment. And certainly
you mustn't blame yourself. But this
young man — dare I ask, Lily, or is it
too personal a question? — are you still
fond of him?'

For a moment I was silent as many
questions raged through my churning

mind. Instinctively I knew that he wanted to know if I was in love with Matt, and if I thought that one day soon I might be giving in my notice as we planned our marriage. But I also knew that would never happen. Yet I must be fair to Matt, who still hoped I might return to him. And then, over and above all these thoughts, one became all-important: I must see Matt and tell him the truth. That our adolescent little romance was over. He would be hurt, I knew, and I felt guilty; yet something deep inside me told me that life was like this, often knocking people over, and then allowing them to recover and find the thing they thought they had lost somewhere else.

Eventually I found the strength to answer the vital question. 'No, Mr Daniel, I don't love Matt. And tomorrow I shall go and find him, and tell him that he must stop bothering me.'

Our eyes met and at once I knew that he was pleased with my answer. Why, I didn't even want to think about; but he

smiled and nodded, and said gently, 'Thank you for telling me, Lily. And of course I will respect what you said. I hope the young man will find someone else, for living without love is a hard and lonely prospect.' He looked at me very directly, adding slowly, 'And you, Lily? May I hope that you, too, will find love — one day?'

What could I say? In my heart words gathered, but I knew they were unspeakable. He was a rich gentleman and I just his daughter's nursemaid. So I managed a forced smile, and somewhere found the courage to say, 'Thank you, Mr Daniel. And of course, I hope that too. But now I really should go up to the nursery — there are several odd jobs I have to do. And so, goodnight.'

I slipped away before he could reply or stop me, and ran up the stairs, shutting myself in the safety of the warm, quiet nursery. I looked in at Mary's bedroom and saw her soundly sleeping, before sitting by the dying fire and trying to find peace in my mind.

This evening had been an extraordinary time and I was grateful to Mr Daniel for talking to me so sensibly, and even encouragingly.

As the time passed, and I realised that I must go to bed, I found the calmness I needed so badly by putting in a few repairing stitches to a coat sleeve Mary had caught on a hook. Busy fingers made me think now of Aunt Edie and her hard work at the bakery, and I started planning our visit there on Tuesday. We would collect the cake, and I hoped that I might hear some news about Dodie, my mother, who we also planned to visit on Wednesday. My birthday. And Mr Daniel was to take us on a picnic.

As I undressed and slipped into bed, I was feeling more sensible, and able to put all the difficult things in my life behind me. Mr Daniel was a kind and sympathetic employer; indeed, he had become a friend. My mother had returned and I had hopes of our relationship becoming more loving and

easy. And Matt? Well, he was a handsome, charming man and I had no doubt now that before long he would find a new love. But it would be hard to tell him how I felt.

And then, almost asleep, a truth became evident. I found myself admitting that I felt a growing love for Daniel. But of course, I would never let him know.

12

The next morning Mrs Hodge waited in the passage after Nancy had cleared the breakfast dishes, and said she had something to ask me. I thought she looked worried, so I smiled and said quietly, 'Yes, Mrs Hodge, what is it?'

She seemed confused. 'Well, miss, when the madam — Mrs Frobisher — left to go to London, we had all the cupboards and larders full of everything we could want over the next week or so. But time goes on, and now I need all sorts of stuff, Miss Lily — why, we're almost out of butter and eggs completely, and your picnic to make ... And when I asked Mr Daniel last night when the madam was coming back, he said he thought she might stay in London a bit longer. So who's going to do the ordering, Miss Lily?' Her eyes were wide and her face

lined with anxiety.

I looked at her, understood her problem, and knew at once that I could help out. 'Don't worry, Mrs Hodge; I'm sure you and I between us can manage to do that. I'll ask Mr Daniel if he agrees; and if so, then we'll make a list at once.'

I went back into the dining room and asked him if I might take the responsibility for keeping Mrs Hodge's requirements ordered and delivered. He looked at me very directly, and a slight frown creased his high forehead as he said, 'But Lily, you have enough to do, I'm sure, without taking on more work. Yes, it's true that my mother thinks she won't return for a month or two, but there will be no trouble about hiring a housekeeper for the time she remains away. I can speak to the agency today.'

I felt an exciting new self-confidence run through me, and I smiled at him. 'No need for that, Mr Daniel. I should be very glad to help Mrs Hodge in any way I can. And so, have I your

permission to take over the household ordering?'

He paused for a long minute, eyes fixed on mine, and then said, with a note of amusement, 'Is there nothing you cannot do, Miss Lily?'

And because I felt the same amusement bubbling up inside me, I said quickly, 'Well, there are certain things, Mr Daniel, that might make me think twice. But ordering sugar and flour and eggs is well within my ability, I think — don't you?'

I had the enjoyment of hearing him laugh heartily as he nodded before striding down the passage and into the hall, where he took his hat from the stand and looked back at me before opening the front door.

'Just make sure you don't overdo all the extra work, please. And make use of Mary's help, if possible. It would be good for her to learn that people have to fetch and carry. I'll see you at luncheon, Lily.' Then he was gone.

We shopped happily that morning, the list Mrs Hodge and I had concocted safely in my hand, and Mary asking question after question as we went from the grocer to the butcher and then on to the greengrocer. We were treated to smiles and — for Mary — the offer of biscuits, chocolates, and even an apple. But I managed to keep her away from such indulgence, saying lightly that Mr Daniel preferred his daughter to remain slender and not get too fat. Laughter followed us as we left the shops and walked home, knowing that the orders would be delivered that same after-noon.

At luncheon Mary told Mr Daniel everything she had seen and heard and learned this morning. He looked at me across the table and said with an amused smile, 'Perhaps we should allow her to do more shopping and have fewer adventures?'

'But we don't want to change her too much, do we, Mr Daniel? She's so bright and warm and sweet-natured.' I

stopped, suddenly feeling I was talking too much.

But he merely nodded and said very quietly, even as he watched her trying to peel an orange, 'All of those attributes, Lily, are being encouraged by your excellent care of her. You must know that.'

I thought hard, remembering all that had been said the previous night, then said carefully, 'I am growing to love Mary, Mr Daniel. My care of her is as simple as that and I am so grateful that you have given me this opportunity to better my life.'

His expression was warm and his voice almost inaudible as he looked into my eyes. 'And has it not occurred to you that you are also bettering the lives of both Mary and myself, Lily? I told you last night, you have made a great difference to my own life. Which is why I hope to have this picnic with you both on your birthday as a small thank-you for all you are doing.'

Mary caught the vital word, *picnic*,

and said quickly, 'Is Mrs Hodge going to fill the picnic basket, Papa? And where shall we have the picnic? In a garden? Or a forest? Or by a river?'

Mr Daniel wiped his mouth, put down his napkin and attended to his daughter. 'It's going to be a surprise, Mary. We shall have our picnic in a place which neither you nor Lily have been to before — but I believe you will like it. No, I'm not going to tell you where. Be patient and then the surprise will be all the better. And now I must get back to the emporium. Excuse me, Lily.' He left the table and soon I heard the front door shut behind him.

Mary got down from her chair and came to my side. 'A surprise! Why, it might even be a picnic on a boat, do you think, Lily?'

'No, I don't, and I certainly hope not. Eating a picnic at sea might not be so easy as you imagine — think of all those waves and currents. No, I think your papa has found a secret place and will share it with us. So let's forget it for

the moment and go upstairs and quietly look at your books. And then later this afternoon we'll have a little walk. Now, off you go.'

Our afternoon walk took us towards the bakery; I was still worrying about Mother and Aunt Edie making friends again, and hoped to hear some news. As I expected, my aunt was resting, sitting quietly in the back room with a cup of tea and her feet propped up on a stool. She looked at me as we entered, smiled at Mary and said, 'Well, come to hear about your ma, have you, Lily? She hasn't been here for a day or two, so I don't know how she's getting on with the flower business. But I'll tell you something.' She fidgeted in her chair, frowned, and look upset. 'That young chit, little Molly Brown, who I hired to do the cleaning — well, she's gone and left. Too hard, she said. Can you imagine? And so I'm left with all the dirty jobs to do as well as the baking, and I'm getting too old for it. Yes, I'm in a real pickle.' But the frown faded

and she smiled at me. 'Don't fancy coming back, do you maid? You were a good, reliable worker.' Slowly she got up, smoothed down her dress and big apron, and went over to a shelf where several tins were piled up. Opening one, she took out a brandy snap and walked towards Mary, standing, listening and staring at us. 'Well, love, try one of these — made specially for you, they were.'

Mary glanced at me, saw me nod my head, and accepted the crisp brown snap. 'Thank you,' she said politely. 'Lily can't come back and work here, Mrs Drew,' she said between large mouthfuls. 'She's helping Mrs Hodge with the shopping, you see. So you'll have to find someone else to do the sweeping, won't you?'

Aunt Edie stifled a snort and caught my eye. 'My word, you're going up in the world, Lily — sounds very nice.' She bent nearer and said, almost under her breath but with a gleam in her eye, 'Aiming to take the house over, are you,

then? So where will it all end, eh?'

A bit shocked by her question and what she must be thinking, I was glad to be spared from having to answer as the door into the bakery opened and my mother came in. There was a silence of a few charged seconds as we all looked at her, until Mary ran to her side and said gleefully, 'Flower lady! We want to come and see your garden again — please may we do so?'

At once the atmosphere changed. My mother — Dodie — put down her baskets and bent down towards Mary, offering her the very last flower, a small pink rose which smelled beautiful. She said quietly, 'I'd love you to come, Miss Mary, but I'm afraid I shan't be there much longer.'

Aunt Edie's face tightened and then slowly softened and she looked at me as if we were partners in some sort of important plan. I smiled encouragingly, feeling that somehow things might be working out between the two sisters, and then my mother looked directly at

my aunt, and said quietly, 'I have to move out of the cottage, Edie, so I wondered if I could come back here. I could help you with all the work, and we could get to know each other again.'

I felt my heart jump with relief; things could be working out! Then I looked at Aunt Edie to see her reaction. Her lined face had become tight, and I guessed that many conflicting thoughts were running around her head: past memories, present days, and what the future might bring. Should she welcome Dodie, or would it all end as it had begun, with bad feelings?

And then, as I watched, it seemed a small miracle was at work. Aunt Edie's face softened and a smile spread, starting slowly and then filling her whole face. Her voice was quiet, softer than usual, as she put out a hand towards my mother and said, 'Well, love, maybe it's time we got together again. Yes, come back and let's see how we get on.'

My mother took the offered hand,

looked at its calloused, red palm, then slowly replied, her own voice almost inaudible, 'I'm so glad, Edie. I hate all these bad feelings. And I'll work hard, I really will.' She turned to look at Mary and me and her smile blossomed, until she was no longer the poor woman who had first sold us flowers, but a new being with bright eyes and a smile that blessed us all. 'Living back in Teignmouth, maybe I'll see you more, Lily — and Miss Mary . . . '

I nodded, unable to speak, and then Aunt Edie went into action, pushing the kettle onto the range and reaching up to find the big brown teapot. 'All right, Dodie, well, you can have the back bedroom that this maid used. When do you think you'll move in?'

Mother pulled a stool from under the table and sank down on it. She smiled as she said, 'I can come this evening, Edie. I'm sorry to leave the cottage of course, but the landlord wants me to go. Something about him selling the big house on the estate further up the lane.

So when we've had that cup of tea you're making, I'll be on my way.' She looked past me towards Mary, who was finishing her sticky brandy snap and wiping fingers on her coat. 'I'm sorry you can't visit the garden, my lover, but perhaps you and Lily and I can go somewhere else and look at flowers now I live nearer — what do you think?'

Mary said, 'Oh yes, that would be lovely. Will it be soon?'

Mother and I smiled at each other. Then I went to the sink in the corner, found a damp cloth, and wiped Mary's sticky fingers. I accepted the mug of tea Aunt Edie had brewed and found another stool — sitting beside Mother, with Mary close to my side, hoping, I imagined, for another brandy snap.

I said, 'Too bad of your landlord to evict you at such short notice, Mother. But I suppose that's how these things work nowadays. I didn't know there was a bigger house attached to the estate — and empty. Perhaps one day we'll wander up the lane and look at it.'

Aunt Edie broke in. 'Landlords, huh! All money and promises, as I see it. Well, you'll be safe enough here, Dodie. And I won't overcharge you for rent!'

We all laughed, and then my birthday cake became the main topic of conversation, with Mary asking to see it. Once it had been produced — a huge, beautiful fruitcake with nuts and cherries all part of it, and Aunt Edie asking Mother if she would like to do the icing — it was time to leave and go home. We parted with smiles; and after some slightly awkward uncertainty, a hug from Mother and a tight-lipped grin from Aunt Edie, Mary and I left the bakery and walked back towards the Esplanade.

Mary skipped along beside me. 'After your mother has done the icing,' she said, 'we must make sure we bring that lovely cake home so that we can have it as part of our picnic.' She looked up at me. 'Aren't you looking forward to it, Lily? Papa taking us to a

secret place, and that great big cake to come with us!' Then she thought for a moment before adding, 'But we'll give Mrs Hodge and Nancy a piece, won't we?'

I said, 'That would be very nice, Mary. And what about Eddie, in the stable? Couldn't he have some, too?'

We reached the back door of Number Three and she stopped suddenly, saying, 'Yes, he can have a small bit — but we want to have lots left for ourselves, don't we, Lily? What a good thing it's such a big cake.'

We went up to the nursery to get ourselves tidy for spending time with Mr Daniel once he came home, and I found I was smiling. Greedy Mary went on and on about the birthday cake, but I just listened and thought how wonderfully well it was all turning out, Aunt Edie and Mother being reunited and even living together again. My feelings for Mother were growing deeper, and I felt all the happier because of it.

Life, I thought as we went down to wait for Mr Daniel in the drawing room, was certainly full of surprises, some good and some bad. What might happen next? I wondered.

13

Mary and I waited for Mr Daniel in the drawing room, looking at an album of photographs that Mrs Frobisher had kept on a small table beside her chair. 'There's Mama,' said Mary suddenly, pointing at the image of a pretty young woman with a charming smile. 'She's gone now . . . ' I saw tears fill her blue eyes.

I put my arms around her, drew her nearer to me and said very quietly, 'But you still have your papa, who loves you so much.'

She nodded, and I wiped away the tears running down her sad face. She looked up at me. 'And you love me, Lily, don't you? More than Nanny Brooks did. She wasn't as nice as you.' A slow smile dawned, and gratefully I hugged her.

'Of course I love you, Mary. And I

love you most when you're being good and quiet.' But I knew this wasn't true. Mary and her willful spirit made me recall what I had been like as a small child. I had enjoyed — although also been worried by — her various adventures. But today she was thinking only of the picnic to come, and not even a word about Becky, who was surely doing something she shouldn't have done.

We continued looking at the photographs. There was one of Mr Daniel several years younger, with his arm around his wife. I felt a chill run through me. Of course I knew the marriage had been a happy one and I was glad for him, but there was something in those black and white figures that made me feel so envious. Would I ever stand next to a man who I loved and who loved me, and who had his arm around me? I was glad when Mary jumped up and ran to the door.

'I can hear Papa! He's home.'

And there he was, coming into the

room and smiling first at Mary and then at me before sinking into his usual chair. 'What a day!' he said. 'We're having a fashion parade on Monday and all the models are fussing about who will wear what, and I shall be glad when it's over. Necessary, of course, as the forerunner of our annual summer sale. Business always keeps one on one's toes. But on Wednesday I shall forget the emporium because it's Lily's birthday and our picnic.'

By now Mary was on his lap, looking up into his face with an adoring smile. She started to tell him about the famous cake, but he stopped her. 'Sweetheart, wait a moment. I'm sure the cake will be a masterpiece, but I have some news for you. Something I think you'll be pleased about.'

She sat up straighter, waiting, eyes wide and shining. 'What is it, Papa?'

He threw me a glance before saying, 'Miss Dulcie Rowan — you remember, she was the dance competition judge — came to see me this morning, asking

if I would allow you to join her weekly dancing class. She thinks you have a certain talent and might do well if you had some instruction. What do you think about that, Mary mine?'

'Yes, yes, Papa! How lovely!' Mary slipped from his lap and began swirling around the room, her smile so broad I could hardly see her eyes. She came up to my chair, paused, and said, 'Did you dance when you were a little girl, Lily? Like me? Like this?' And off she went, toes pointed, arms gracefully floating as she danced back to Mr Daniel's chair.

I said, 'Why yes, Mary — I went to a barn dance once, with Matt.' I hadn't meant to bring him into the conversation, but the memory was a strong one. I tried to think of something else. 'And Jess and I went to the tea dances in the village hall a few times. It was great fun, and we loved the music and fussed about our dresses.'

Mr Daniel looked at me and I felt colour spread over my face. His eyes were keen and I felt they could see into

my mind. 'So you think it would be beneficial for Mary to have lessons, Lily? I need your agreement before I actually decide, you see. And — ' Here he leaned forward, his voice quieter. ' — it would prepare her for starting school in the autumn, don't you think?'

I thought, and knew I must agree. Yes, Mary was growing up. Soon she would be out of the nursery and into a new life of dance and general education. And wouldn't need me . . .

I cleared my throat, held my head an inch higher, and met his dark, enquiring eyes. 'Yes, Mr Daniel, I do agree. We must start by doing things slowly, and I think a dance class every week would be the first step.'

He sat back, but still fixed his eyes on mine. He nodded and said, 'Thank you. I knew you would be sensible about it. And so this will be Mary's first step into the outside world; I feel sure she will enjoy the lessons.' Getting up, he drew Mary towards him and said, bending down, 'And now I think we

must go and see Mrs Hodge and ask just what she is preparing for that famous picnic. Come along, Mary.'

Laughing together, Mary chattering about the cake, they left the room. But I stayed where I was, sitting rather stiff and unhappy in Mrs Frobisher's armchair and wondering if this was another of life's little knocks, coming out of the blue, and making me accept all that happened, even when it seemed rather shadowy. As I sat there, Matt's name ran around my mind. I had just put him there, and I knew the time had come when I must go and talk to him. Perhaps on Sunday afternoon, after we had been to church, and in the afternoon Mr Daniel and Mary usually went out together, giving me time to myself. Yes, I would walk around to the river beach and see if I could find him.

Sunday was a day of grey clouds and chilling showers of rain. We went to church and then, after Mr Daniel and Mary had gone to visit friends, I ventured out to the river beach. As I

had thought, few fishing boats were out of the harbour today, with the sea rolling ferociously and the wind sharpening. And yes, there by his hut was Matt, sitting just inside the open doorway mending nets.

I paused for a few nervous minutes before approaching him. He looked up, put the net down on the floor, and stood up without a greeting. It was up to me, I realised, to start the conversation; one that I feared would be unsettling for both of us.

Surprisingly, after that short silence, he smiled a bit warily and said, 'Good to see you, Lily. And you're in time for a cup of tea. The kettle's been singing for the last five minutes. Come in, sit down.'

I sat down in the rickety chair he had vacated and stared out onto the river. Today it was grey-green and running fast as if in a hurry to get out there and join the heaving ocean. I thought about the dangers of life at sea, and then thanked goodness that Matt, and most

of the other local men, hadn't taken out their boats. When Matt offered me a mug of steaming tea I was able to smile and murmur, 'Thank you, and I think we need to talk, don't we?' I was glad to see him nod, then pull out a canvas chair and sit down, nursing his own mug of tea.

We drank in silence, joined only by a few glances at one another. He spoke first. 'A dirty day, better in here than out on the water. And there's always nets to mend.'

'Yes.' How could I make him understand that I still had affection for him, but not one that would develop the way he hoped? Then I remembered telling Mary about the barn dance, and at once the words came. 'I told Miss Mary about the barn dance you took me to, Matt — one of your friends living on a farm near Bishop — and what fun it was.' I smiled across the small space, and was glad to see him returning it.

'Billy Boyne, his pa's farm. Yes, those

barn dances — rough and ready, hot and hard work, but enjoyable.' He stopped, put down his mug and looked at me very directly. 'Those were the days. I had you in my arms — I even kissed you in a shadowy corner one evening — and you didn't say no, did you, Lily?'

I knew the difficult bit was here. I met his eyes and took a deep breath. 'No, Matt, that young Lily had no other thoughts but to have a good time, and a handsome boy to go out with. Yes, I did kiss you, and enjoyed it. But now . . . well, I've said it before. Things are different. And I ask you to accept it. I work for the Frobishers and I hope to keep my situation, which will enable me to live simply but without undue poverty, once Miss Mary no longer needs me.' I stopped. I had said it all, and nothing else could help. I looked at him again, a long look taking in his untidy hair, his shabby clothes, and his big hands which had been strong and cajoling on the days when we hopped,

skipped and jumped at the barn dance. Now he was different from the young boy: a mature man who had experienced danger and hardship in his chosen trade. There was a big void between us. I said firmly, 'Do you see, Matt?'

There was a long moment's silence when I could almost hear the thoughts of both of us churning around. But then he began to smile — that magical lift of the lips which had always shown his feelings. 'I see, Lily. And so that's how it's got to be, is it? I understand what you're saying and how important it is to keep your position; but I shall go on hoping. You see, to me you'll always be the same Lily, even though you dress more smartly and talk better than you used to. I still want you. So go your own way, lover, but just know I'll always be there, watching, and hoping.'

No more words. The wind swirled along the waves in the river, gulls shrieked, and somewhere a dog barked. We sat and looked at each other until

he said, 'More tea?'

I shook my head and got up. 'No thanks, Matt. I must go. I just wanted to get things straight between us.'

'Yes,' he said, rising and standing by me in the open doorway. 'Well, they're straight enough. Not what you want, Lily, but it's how they are. So I'll see you around, and I hope you'll come to me if ever you need anything that Mr Frobisher can't offer you.'

I didn't like that. As if Mr Daniel was buying me. Was that what he really thought? But no good to argue. I did up my coat, pulled my hat down more firmly, and stepped out onto the sandy beach. I looked over my shoulder and saw the determination in his weather-tanned face. 'Goodbye, Matt,' I said, and walked quickly away, glad to get back to the town and the house at Number Three the Esplanade, which suddenly seemed a real home. Alone in my bedroom, I sat quietly, thinking about that conversation, until I heard voices downstairs and realised Mr

Daniel and Mary had returned. Then I went down and joined them, and Matt drifted out of my thoughts.

*　*　*

On Monday morning Mr Daniel had his breakfast in a hurry. He seemed tense, I thought, and it didn't help him that Mary followed him into the hall and kept asking him something, amid bursts of giggling. I called her back, and slowly she came with him just behind her. He looked at me without a smile, saying, 'Mary would like to come and watch the dress parade this morning, Lily. It starts at eleven o'clock, but be there a little earlier so that you can get seats. Now I must rush.'

I was surprised, to say the least. So whatever Mary wanted, she must have, which wasn't good for a small child. But I could do nothing except be sure that we were at the emporium in good time, our clothes neat and tidy, and Mary as serious as she could ever be

expected to be. The atmosphere in the big dress department at the top of the building was warm and exciting, and from somewhere soft music played. Customers were filling the gilt chairs surrounding the small circular stage in the middle, and curtains hung at the back of the room behind which, I supposed, the models were dressing.

Mary was surprisingly quiet and good. I saw she kept her eyes on the curtains, and when finally they opened she caught her breath as if waiting for something special. The models, all sales girls, looked most attractive, their coiffeurs in keeping with the lovely clothes they showed off. At first there were walking-suits in different materials, and I particularly liked the dove-grey one which I could imagine being paired with a large hat decorated with flowers. But not for me. I knew I was lucky to be dressed neatly in a good-quality nurse's uniform. I would never wear such beautiful clothes.

The chatter of the audience quietened as the mood changed, and after a slight pause the models appeared again in ball gowns and dinner dresses. I heard intakes of admiring breath, and even a murmured 'Oh, how lovely!' as the girls walked slowly and twirled before disappearing behind the curtains.

At the end the chatter returned, with a lot of fidgeting and ladies turning to each other and discussing the clothes. Mary tugged at my arm. 'Did you like them, Lily? Which did you like best? I liked the yellow one with the big sash and the flounces around the hem — did you like it?'

I smiled at her, preparing to get up and have our usual morning walk along the Esplanade before returning home for luncheon. 'Yes, it was lovely, Mary; I liked it very much. But come along now, and perhaps we'll call in at the Seaspray Café before we go home.' I felt I needed to talk to Jess about Matt, but as we left the big upstairs

department, Mr Daniel came to my side.

'Did you enjoy the show? I thought the girls did very well.'

Mary wriggled and pulled at his hand. 'And Lily liked the yellow one, Papa. So did I — very spec — ' She frowned, struggling with the long word, then grinned. 'Spectacular! There, I said it!'

Mr Daniel and I laughed, and I thought that she definitely was ready for school in the autumn. Was there a local one where she would be happy? And what would I do when she was out all day?

But this wasn't the moment to start worrying. I said, 'Thank you so much for inviting us, Mr Daniel. I thought it was a wonderful show, and I hope it does the business a lot of good. And now we must leave you in peace.'

Mary burst in. 'We're going to the café, Papa, and I shall have one of those nice biscuits Jess makes.'

He nodded and we smiled at each

other. Then I led her down and out of the emporium and along the seafront, where the waves curled lacy scallops on the golden sand, and I thought how lucky I was to be here with an employer who was such a wonderful man. And for the moment I quite forgot Matt.

14

Jess looked at me with her sharp, penetrating eyes. 'Poor Matt's unhappy,' she said while wiping down a table top, then gesturing for me to sit down. 'Mary, here's your biscuit, and now go and see what you can find to play with in the tin cupboard, maid.' Off went Mary to pull out cake and patty tins and start to build things with them.

I said, 'Did Matt tell you he was unhappy? When was that?'

'Yesterday, after you'd gone home. He came in for a chat, like he does sometimes.'

Something made my brain work overtime. 'You mean, he comes in to see you?'

Jess paused a moment and I saw her cheeks colour up. 'Well, yes. Not often, but . . . sometimes. Needs someone to talk to, he says. And I like to see him.'

It was becoming clear. Matt would offload all his troubles on poor Jess who, as I knew from the past, had always admired him, even though he paid her little attention. Now, it seemed, she was filling my place in his life. I had to admit I was pleased.

I said gently, 'You have my permission to fall for Matt, if that's what you want. He understands that I'm living a different life now, and I'm sure he'll be glad of a new friend to fill the gap.' I smiled and, reassured, I watched her smile, too.

She got up from the table, hurrying into the kitchen and suddenly becoming very busy. 'Can't stop for more talk,' she called over her shoulder. 'Got a couple coming in for lunch, and I must start preparing the food. Sorry, but you'll have to go, Lily.'

I nodded, got up, helped Mary put all the tins back in the cupboard. Then, before leaving Jess at the oven stirring something, I said quietly, 'Good luck, Jess. And don't think badly of me, will

you? Like Matt, please try and understand that my life has taken a different
turning now. But I hope we'll always be
friends?'

She turned, smiled over her shoulder,
nodded and said quickly, 'Nothing'll
change that, Lily.'

Her warm smile stayed in my mind
as Mary and I left the café, walking
back towards home and luncheon.

* * *

Mr Daniel was late for luncheon and I
thought he looked harassed, his lean
face showing lines that weren't usually
there. But he smiled as he finally joined
us at the table. Mary was chattering as
she ate her soup and I gently reminded
her that meals were for eating, not
talking. She looked at me with a pout,
but Mr Daniel put his hand on hers
and said, 'You and I will have a little
chat before I go back this afternoon,
Mary. So eat up slowly now, please.'

I wanted to say something to him as

he left the dining room after a short rest with the newspaper, on his way back to the Emporium, but knew it wasn't my place. Of course I couldn't say that I wished he didn't work so hard, and that I thought he looked really tired. But the words were all there, running around in my mind, even as I watched him go into the hall and talk quietly to Mary before leaving the house and striding rapidly up the road, disappearing into the distance. Perhaps, I thought, when Mrs Frobisher returned, she would see how weary he was and give him some maternal and possibly acceptable advice. I sighed, wishing I could help; but as a nursemaid, what could I do?

Mary and I stayed at home that afternoon, as the rain came down more heavily, and I had to wrack my brains with stories about Becky to keep her amused. At tea time she asked, 'When Becky is on her boat, what does she do when it rains?' That gave me great ideas for describing the little girl wearing

huge oilskins and a sou'wester. This amused Mary to the extent that we then had to get an old newspaper and make a copy of what we both thought a sou'wester looked like.

Laughter filled the house later, going down to spend time with Mr Daniel after his return from the emporium. I was glad to see how his face lightened as Mary spun her adventurous web of what Becky was doing.

'Let's leave Becky on her boat, shall we?' he asked, with a grin in my direction. 'And make plans for the birthday picnic. I've ordered a sunny day. Mrs Hodge is making sausage rolls and jellies and other wonderful things, and we'll take a flask of tea and some lemonade for you, Mary mine.'

She sat beside his chair for a moment, quite still, with her face turned up to him. Then she said, 'Will there be flowers in the secret place, Papa? I do hope so. Lily said she will teach me how to make a daisy chain, you see.'

Mr Daniel looked at me and suddenly I could read his face. He was pleased with me; he was glad I was here; he thought I was the right person to help bring up his daughter. I felt my emotions swell, rise to the surface, and almost break out either in tears or joyous laughter. But somehow I controlled them, simply smiled at him, and said a bit unsteadily, 'Every little girl should know how to do that, don't you think?'

He kept looking at me, and I watched how his straight lips slowly curved into an easy smile, as he nodded and said very quietly, 'Yes, Lily, I do.'

The next morning Nancy, the housemaid, met me in the passage as I was going upstairs. She looked worried. 'Oh, Miss Lily, I don't know what to do about the madam's bedroom. She's going to be away a bit longer, Mr Daniel told me, and I think it needs a bit of attention. What do you think I should do?'

I was surprised. No one had

suggested I might act as housekeeper as well as nursemaid. Certainly, I was helping Mrs Hodge with the ordering, but here was Nancy wanting help as well.

I thought for a moment, then said, 'Let's go and have a look at the room, shall we?'

Mrs Frobisher's bedroom was large, at the front of the house, with big windows looking out over the seafront. It smelled a bit musty, so I thought opening a window might help. 'A good dusting, Nancy, I think. And what about changing the bed sheets? And putting some dried lavender under the pillows? I think I can get some for you.'

At once my mind went back to my mother, who grew lavender in huge bushes. Mary and I would go to the bakery this afternoon and ask for some. And, of course, I was anxious to see how Aunt Edie and Mother were getting on. Nancy's worried face cleared, and at once she started doing as I had suggested.

'The madam's a long time away,' she said, 'and I don't always know what to do next. I mean, I don't like to bother Mr Daniel every day.'

I smiled at her. 'I'll always help if I can, Nancy. Between us we'll probably keep the house going until the madam comes back again.' She looked reassured and at once started stripping the bed. I went on up to the nursery, thinking with amusement how I now seemed to be in charge of Number Three the Esplanade, not just the lowly nervous nursemaid who had first come here. But the feeling was a good one, making me understand that I was capable of more things than I had ever imagined. And, of course, I was helping Mr Daniel by taking on all these new tasks. I recalled the expression on his face earlier last night, and felt a great warmth spread through me. Life was good these days.

Mary and I walked to the bakery that afternoon and found Mother and Aunt Edie at work, a lot of flour spread all

over the floor, and their two faces red from the heat and the exertions. But they looked up and smiled as we opened the door and went in. Mother put down the rag with which she was wiping empty shelves and came towards us. 'How lovely to see you,' she said, and I knew she wanted to kiss me, but I stepped back. I wasn't ready for such open feelings — not yet. Her smile faded a little, but she bent to Mary and asked, 'Have you come to collect that birthday cake, Miss Mary?'

'Yes, yes,' said Mary excitedly. 'Have you done the icing? Does it look pretty? Will it taste nice?'

Aunt Edie's voice reached us from the big oven where she was taking new loaves out with the long paddle. 'It's a good one, maid. You'll enjoy all that chocolate icing and the sugar flowers we've put on it. Just don't eat it all at once, will you? But you'll have to wait a few minutes while I get this job finished, and then Dodie and I will put it in a box for you to carry home.'

I nodded and we sat down quietly, me on the one hard chair by the window and Mary at my side, eyes wide as she watched the two women going about their work. When Mother had finished wiping the shelves she came over to me and said very quietly, 'I think Edie is pleased I'm here to help, but of course we have our differences. Neither of us is going to change all at once, so we must just go on and see what happens.'

'Yes, I see. And that seems sensible.' And hopeful, I thought. And then I remembered the lavender. 'Mother, have you any lavender in your garden? I should love to have some to dry and put into bags — they're very good for airing sheets and clothes.'

Her face clouded. 'Yes, of course, Lily. Lots of lavender there, but it's not my home any longer so I can't pick any more flowers, can I?'

I frowned. 'I think your landlord is being very unkind, giving you such short notice. Who is he, Mother?'

She said nothing for a moment, and I saw her face grow tense. 'A Mr Briggs, one of the town councillors. But you see, he's sold the estate and so of course I had to go. I'm sorry about the flowers, and I shall miss growing them. But Edie and I are getting used to each other, so perhaps everything is turning out for the best.'

I nodded. It seemed to me far from the best that Mother should have to give up her beloved flowers, but what could I do about it? At least she seemed happy enough to be here in the bakery, and I knew I would try hard be a good daughter now that we had come together again. By now Aunt Edie had helped Mother put the new loaves on the shelves, and she came to me, smiling. 'Well, lover, your birthday tomorrow, and I wish you many happy returns. Your ma and I are gradually getting used to being together again, and I'll say this for her — she's a bit slow, but she's a good worker!'

We had a laugh then, and Aunt Edie

produced a big box into which the wonderful cake was carefully packed. I picked it up, told Mary to button her coat, and said a smiling goodbye to Mother and her sister, who watched us as we slowly left the bakery and walked up the road, going home.

And there was Matt, coming out of the Seascape Café as we passed it. He stopped, stared at me, coloured, and then muttered something about 'Hope you have a good birthday tomorrow, Lily' before swinging away and going around the corner.

Mary had watched him and now she turned to me, her small face full of an expression of childish understanding that made me realise how she was growing up. 'He's nicer now,' she said. 'Is that because he went to see Jess in the café? I want to give him a piece of your cake, but I suppose I can't, can I? Oh well, come on, Lily, let's hurry and get home and show the cake to Mrs Hodge and Nancy and Papa when he comes back. And tell them it mustn't be

cut until tomorrow. Oh, it'll be your birthday soon, Lily!' She did a little jiggy dance at my side, looking up at me with those wide sky-blue eyes, small face full of excitement. 'Isn't it all lovely?' she cried, and I thought, *Yes it is, but do I really deserve such loveliness in my life?*

Back in the nursery, after leaving the cake in the kitchen amid admiring looks from Mrs Hodge and Nancy — and strict instructions from Mary not to cut it until tomorrow — I settled her down with a new colouring book and some crayons while I sat by the fire and let my thoughts unwrap themselves.

My twentieth birthday tomorrow, and a picnic in the afternoon with Mary and Mr Daniel. And a secret place to explore. And, as I watched the flames in the fire flickering brightly, I somehow knew that tomorrow was going to be a special day. Very special, but in some way that I couldn't possibly imagine at the moment.

15

Sun shone through the curtains as I awoke, and I smiled at the thoughts whirling around in my head. My birthday! And a picnic to look forward to. But first I had to deal with Mary's excitement.

'Happy birthday, Lily,' she cried as I tried to dress her. Standing on tiptoe, she reached up and kissed me. 'Hurry up, let's go downstairs because — oh!' She giggled, then put a hand over her mouth. 'Just wait and see!'

Downstairs Mrs Hodge waited at the bottom of the staircase, her smile concealing the lines and wrinkles. 'Happy birthday, Miss Lily — and a lady just brought this for you. She wouldn't stay, but said you would understand.'

I took the small posy she handed me. No, not lavender, but tiny blue flowers.

I murmured, 'Forget-me-nots. Thank you, Mother. No, I'll never forget.'

The morning was full of excitement, with Mary rushing into the hall after breakfast to see if the postman had been. He had, but only to being letters for Mr Daniel. Why should I wish for someone to send me something? I had to discipline myself very carefully, for the day had something about it which excited me almost as much as it did young Mary.

She and I were upstairs and Mr Daniel in the hall taking his hat off the stand when there was a knock at the door. He opened it and I heard a smile in his voice as he said, 'Ah yes, Mrs Burton. You're in good time. Thank you so much — and I'll see you later at the emporium.'

It was impossible to control Mary, who turned and rushed downstairs so fast I thought she might fall. But no, she landed safely, and grabbed at her Papa's arm. 'Can I carry it?' she implored.

He laughed, looking over her head at me as he said, 'Better let Lily take her present herself I think, Mary — but I'm sure she'll let you help her open it.' Coming to the bottom of the staircase, he added, 'This is Mary's birthday present to you, Lily. We hope very much that you'll like it.' He put the large brown paper parcel into my arms and added very quietly, his smile warm and easy, 'Please wear it when we have dinner tonight. That's when we'll really celebrate your birthday. And now I must rush.' He gave Mary a last hug, put on his hat, gave us a wave, and left the house.

Upstairs the parcel was quickly undone, and to my amazement a beautiful gown lay there among the tissue-paper wrappings. I took a huge breath, looked at Mary, saw her shining eyes and the expectation on her face, and said everything that was in my mind.

'It's lovely, so lovely. Oh Mary, it's the gown we admired at your papa's

dress parade, isn't it? The one you asked if I really liked. So that's why you wanted to know — and you've given it to me!' I caught her up in my arms and hugged her until she squeaked and laughed.

'I can't breathe! Let me go, Lily, and try on this dress, please. Put it on, quick, quick!'

I felt tears pricking behind my eyes as knowledge came. Yes, Mary had chosen this wonderful present to give me, but it must have been Mr Daniel who agreed, who had ordered Mrs Burton to deliver it first thing this morning. And what had he said before he left — so quietly, and with such an expression of warmth? 'Wear it for dinner — when we'll really celebrate your birthday.' My heartbeat was returning to its normal rate now and I blinked away the tears, for something warmer and much more exciting was there in my dreams. Mr Daniel and I would have dinner together. I would appear different, in my new gown. Was I always to be just

the nursemaid looking after his little girl? I knew now that I loved Mary as if she were my own; I controlled the household staff here and had become a capable manager; and I knew, too, that I had fallen in love with Daniel.

But dreams rarely came true, and slowly I slid down to earth as I hung up the new gown and let Mary help me take off my big white apron and dark dress. Then I carefully slipped into the richness of the beautiful dress.

She stood back, her face full of amazement. 'You look all different, Lily,' she said in her small voice. 'You look . . . lovely.'

I bent down to her and looked into those wide sky-blue eyes and whispered, 'If I do look lovely, Mary, it's all because of you — and not just the gown. Because I think you love me, like I love you.' I stopped, because I guessed what I wanted her to say, and it could never be.

As if she read my mind, she said with a huge smile, 'And Papa loves us, too,

Lily. Both of us, doesn't he?'

All I could say was a wavering, 'I hope so, Mary. I do hope so.'

She started dancing around the room. 'Now we must get ready for the picnic! You can't wear that, Lily, can you? It might get all crushed and dirty in the trap — so take it off and hang it up, and we'll go and see if Mrs Hodge has got the picnic all ready for us.'

The gown looked so elegant, hanging up by the wardrobe, and I stood there for a few minutes admiring it: a soft ivory colour with tight sleeves, a low neck and the collar trimmed with gold, the same as the belt that encircled the tiny waist. And then froths of flounces, broderie anglaise, and lace falling down the skirt, emphasising the tiny bustle at the back, which was held in place with a huge bow of golden ribbon. In my mind I could hear the various rich materials singing and shushing as the wearer moved — as I would, that evening. But then I had the sense to try and think of

other things; to remember that the morning held a few tasks we must not forget.

Out in the clear morning air we walked briskly down the seafront, calling in at the Seaspray Café to say hello to Jess, who smiled and said, 'Happy birthday, Lily! You look as if you're having a good day. Where are you off to, then?'

I said, 'To see my mother and my aunt, and to thank them for all the good things they've done for me during my life. Can't stop, Jess, but we'll come and tell you the rest of it another day.' And off we went to the bakery.

Mother and Aunt Edie were all smiles. Mother hugged Mary and then looked at me, wondering. I remembered the forget-me-nots and put my arms around her. 'Thank you,' I whispered. 'And of course I never will forget, Mother.'

She kissed me on the cheek, then smiled as she said unsteadily, 'I got up early and walked back to the cottage to

pick the flowers. I hope the new owner won't mind.'

Aunt Edie looked at me very keenly and said, 'What're you doing to celebrate, then, maid?'

'Mr Daniel has arranged a picnic tea,' I answered. 'And a secret place to go to. It's all very exciting.'

They both nodded, and I wondered what either of them would say if they knew that I was dining alone with Mr Daniel this evening in the beautiful new gown which he — although Mary said it was her present — had given me.

What an exciting morning! I thought Mary needed a short rest before luncheon and the afternoon's outing, so we returned to the nursery and sat quietly, Mary making up a new story about Becky, the girl on the boat who loved chocolate and was always asking for some. Then we had luncheon with Mr Daniel and made preparations for the great picnic.

Mrs Hodge loaded a large hamper into the back of the trap when Eddie

brought it round to the back door, and Nancy added the box with the famous cake in it along with a knife, some plates, and napkins in case we covered ourselves in chocolate. Eddie said, 'I'll bring Duchess round to the front, miss, an' then you can go off from there.'

Mr Daniel waited for us in the hall, his black suit changed for a tweedy jacket and a cream shirt, and I thought he looked handsomer than ever. We climbed into the trap, Mr Daniel replacing Eddie in the driving seat, with Mary beside him, while I looked after the hamper in the back.

We trotted quietly through the town and then into the surrounding countryside along Bishop Road, past the track leading to Mother's cottage, and then on down a side road, eventually reaching a large house standing alone in the winding lane, surrounded by trees, and with the river not far away. It was quiet and very beautiful.

Mr Daniel turned and looked at me and said, 'Here we are, Lily. Take a

good look around, will you? Because there's something I have to tell you.'

I felt instinctively that this was the place he had in mind for our picnic; and that there was, indeed, a secret to be discovered here.

As soon as he had halted the trap and hitched Duchess to a nearby tree, with plenty of grass to graze, Mary took my hand and said, 'Are we going in the big house?' I looked at Mr Daniel for his reply.

He nodded and said, 'We'll do the exploring first, shall we? And then the picnic. Mary, take Lily's hand and come with me.' He produced a key from his pocket and unlocked the front door. 'I expect it'll smell a bit musty; no one has lived here for a while. Be careful where you tread.'

Slowly we entered, and at once I felt the warmth and happiness of this old house reaching out to welcome us. We passed through the hall, with its floor of white-and-black squares, and went down a passage into a large, spacious

room which had floor-length windows and a big granite fireplace. Yes, it smelt unlived-in, and the grate was full of sticks and rubbish and dust; but I knew all this would be cleaned up and come alive once someone decided to live here again.

Something warm and wanting spread through me. I knew instinctively that to live here would be a wonderful gift. I sighed and hoped the new owner, when one appeared, would respect and love this old house.

Mr Daniel had heard my sigh. He turned from inspecting the elm floor-boards beneath the windows and said, 'What do you think, Lily? Could this old place be turned into a living family home again?'

'Yes,' I said at once. 'It seems to be a lonely place now, but once it's got people living in it, I'm sure it will be beautiful again.'

He let Mary run around the room, touching everything she saw, before coming to my side. 'I think you're

right,' was all he said, but I saw from his expression that he was pleased with my answer. He smiled and nodded. Then, as he walked back to the door, he said, 'Let's go and look upstairs, shall we?'

We all trooped up the elegant oak staircase where the dust lay thick on the balusters. A big bedroom opened off the landing, with windows looking down over the neglected garden. Mary found mouse droppings on the window seat, and I imagined a huge bed covered with creamy linen to match floral curtains which would give the room a sense of the flowers which the tidied garden would produce.

Mary was rushing down the passage, exploring each room she passed. 'There's one for me!' she called as Mr Daniel and I joined her. 'Not a nursery, because I'm a big girl now, but my own little bedroom!' She stopped suddenly, looked at me, and said more quietly, 'And where will you sleep, Lily? Will you have a bedroom, too?'

To my surprise, just as I was about to

answer, Mr Daniel took her hand and led her down the stairs. 'Come along,' he said, looking back over his shoulder. 'I think we must find a convenient spot for our picnic, so let's look at the garden now.'

Then we were outside in the sunshine, leaving the house behind; and, I sensed, leaving some unanswered questions inside it. Where, indeed, would my room be if Mr Daniel decided to buy this house? Was he thinking of doing so? But of course, it was all my imagination; and now we must think about the place for our picnic.

Mr Daniel led us down the path between thick, untidy shrubs and trees, and along a weedy track that left the garden, joining a grassy track down which we walked. I wondered what we should find at the end of it.

And there stood Rose Cottage. I stopped quite still and gasped.

Mary started to giggle, saying, 'It's the flower lady's home!'

Mr Daniel put his hand on my arm. 'What is it, Lily? What's bothering you?'

I had to take a deep breath before I could answer, for uneasy thoughts were circling in my brain, causing confusion. At last I said, 'I'm quite all right, Mr Daniel, but this is the cottage where my Mother lived until she was evicted a few days ago. It's a shock to see it's part of the big house. And I wonder who it was who lived here and turned her out.'

He was silent, just standing, looking at me. I saw how his eyes widened, and an expression of confusion filled his own face. 'Your mother, Lily? The one who left you, and who has now returned? And she lived here? But where is she now?'

'Living with my aunt at the bakery,' I said dully. 'But she can't grow her flowers anymore.' I looked at him very directly, for suddenly the answers to all sorts of queries were beginning to make sense. 'Is this the secret, Mr Daniel? Are you thinking of buying this estate?'

For a long moment he said nothing.

Then he looked across the garden to where Mary had found the little stream and was sitting beside it, intent on seeing a fish. He smiled and said quietly, 'She is happy here.' Turning to me, he took a deep breath and asked, 'But you see, the answer to your question, Lily, depends entirely on you.'

While I tried to sort out just what he could mean, he took my hand and led me, speechless, towards the chair outside the cottage, where I had sat with Mother. 'Sit down here,' he said lightly, 'and I'll bring the hamper along. I'm sure Mary is ready to cut your cake.'

16

What a feast we had, sitting outside the cottage in the sunshine, Mrs Hodge's hamper spread out on the small table in front of us. There were jellies, sandwiches, tarts, sausage rolls — and then Aunt Edie's wonderful cake, covered in chocolate icing with sugared flowers and silver balls decorating it. Mary was in heaven, asking for a second helping, and then pouting when Mr Daniel gently said, 'Leave some for tomorrow, my love. You've eaten quite enough, so why not go and look for those fish again? Lily and I will stay here for a while.'

We watched her run down the path and settle herself by the little stream. I knew then that Daniel had something important to say, and this would be the moment. I sat up very straight and waited.

He poured second cups of tea from the big flask, and then sat back in his canvas chair and looked at me. 'You asked me if I intended to buy this estate, Lily — and the answer is yes. You see, my mother and my brother, Paul, have written to say they will be returning home next month, when Paul plans to come into the business with me. He will certainly be a great help, as I find running the emporium on my own a lot of hard work.'

I nodded. This seemed a good idea, and would allow him more time away from the business. He would, hopefully, look less drawn and weary. And of course he wanted his own home, away from the younger brother and their mother. So this house — neglected and quiet in its countryside surroundings — was to be his and Mary's new home. At once I felt a knot form inside me. And where would I go? Looking for a new situation as a nursemaid, I thought wretchedly.

I met his gaze and said a little

unsteadily, 'And Mary will go to school. There is a very good one in Bishop, I think, not far away. So . . . ' I stopped. The words were hard to say. 'So she will no longer need a nursemaid. But perhaps you will hire someone to manage your new home, who will help look after her.' I looked away from him, for there was something in his dark eyes that I didn't understand. Could it be that here, in this lovely spot, he was going to tell me I was no longer needed?

He reached across the table, leaned over it, took my hand in his and forced me to meet his penetrating gaze. 'Lily, you must know that I don't want you to go. Although it's been a short time that you've been with Mary and me, surely you understand how we rely on you? How Mary loves you? And I . . . ' He stopped abruptly, released my hand, stood up and began slowly walking up and down the path, no longer looking at me. His voice when he spoke again was firmer, more down to earth. 'As you

suggest, I shall need someone to manage the new house.' Turning, he looked down at me. 'Would you care to be that person, Lily? You see . . . ' He cut off the words and frowned. Then he came back to his chair and sat down, and I saw his expression change again. Quietly, he said, 'But perhaps this isn't the time to talk about the future. After all, there's a lot to think about — for both of us. So let's just enjoy being here, shall we? And why don't we join Mary and get a glimpse of this invisible fish?'

I thought I heard amusement in the last words, and felt a tightening of my body as I got to my feet. My thoughts were restless; I needed to know exactly what he expected of me. But no, he was laughing with Mary down by the stream, so I got up and carefully repacked the hamper with the remains of Mrs Hodge's feast.

After another walk around the neglected garden of the empty house, we drove back in the trap, with Mary

yawning and ready, I was sure, for a rest in the quiet nursery. I took her upstairs, aware that Mr Daniel was standing down in the hall, watching us. At the top of the stairs I turned and met his gaze.

He smiled and called up to me, 'Dinner tonight, Lily, and you in your new gown. I look forward to it. And one more surprise.'

I nodded, too tired out with conflicting emotions to answer. Another surprise? And would it be a happy one? I wondered wryly. Or, of course, it could well be my dismissal.

★ ★ ★

Back in the nursery Mary went to bed, tired out and almost instantly asleep. I dressed myself with care, ready for dinner with Mr Daniel. The new gown felt wonderful as I slipped it on. I had brushed my hair until it shone, rolled it into a neater and more becoming style than I usually bothered with, and now I

219

told myself I must look in a long mirror in one of the bedrooms along the passage and see if I looked ready to go downstairs.

Sunlight filled Mrs Frobisher's big bedroom and I wondered, amused, what she would say if she knew I was in there, admiring myself in her cheval mirror. The fragrance of the small bunch of lavender I had picked in Mother's garden before we drove home filled the air as I laid it on the dressing table. Tomorrow I would slip some under the pillows on the bed to welcome Mrs Frobisher home; but now the important thing was to look at myself.

I took a deep breath, stood by the mirror and saw a tall girl with shining hair and an expression of muted excitement mixed with happiness. The gown fell about me in gracious sweeps of rich, elegant cream-coloured material, and the gold trimmings matched the streaks of brilliant sunlight to the light in my eyes.

I moved and heard the swish of lace- and satin-lined flounces, and said very quietly and slowly, hearing in my few words exactly what I was truly thinking, 'Lily Ross, you look very pretty. I do hope Daniel thinks so, too.' Then with a newfound confidence I left the room, closed the door and walked down the curving staircase.

He was there in the hall waiting for me, his smile widening as his eyes met mine. When I reached the bottom step he came to me, holding out his hand, taking mine and saying very quietly, 'Lily, you look lovely.' Inside me I felt all the worry about the future disappear, for now I knew nothing mattered except being here with Daniel, the two of us together, for an evening which I sensed would be unforgettable.

I can hardly recall what we had for dinner, except that Mrs Hodge's cooking was, as usual, wonderful; but I had little appetite. I sipped the wine Daniel poured, and waited for him to tell me what was on his mind.

At first he spoke about the neglected house — how it would need restoring and renovating, and he hoped that I would agree. 'It will make a beautiful family home — don't you think so, Lily?'

I swallowed the lump forming in my throat and took another sip of wine. 'Yes,' I said. 'It will. A new home for you and Mary.'

He pushed aside his empty plate and stood up, looking at me with eyes that I thought held a message of some sort. 'And you, Lily. Our home won't be complete unless you're there.' His voice was quiet but vibrant. I heard the emotion in the words and watched how his smile grew as he added, 'And that's what we have to talk about.'

I said nothing. The old anxiety flooded through me, and I wasn't sure what he expected of me. Was he talking about my becoming his housekeeper in the new house once it was restored? I sat quite still, looking down at the damask tablecloth and wondering how

I could answer him.

But then, moving quickly, he was behind my chair, helping me to clear my skirt as I stood up. 'Lily,' he said very quietly, drawing me around to face him, 'I have something to ask you, but let's go into the drawing room. Mrs Hodge will bring coffee later, and I've arranged for some music to entertain us. You see, I want you to remember this birthday in years to come.' He took my arm, linked it with his and carefully led me away from the table.

In the drawing room I heard the soft tones of the famous 'Blue Danube Waltz' — the one that had been played at the dress parade at the emporium. Then I saw the gramophone and turned to him. He was smiling as if pleased with a new toy. I said, 'So this is the other surprise you talked about, Mr Daniel — isn't that so?'

'Yes, it is. And I hope you're pleased. I wanted music especially, Lily, because I remember you saying you loved to dance. And I hope . . . ' He stopped,

drew me a step closer, and then said, so softly that I could only just hear the words, 'May I have the honour of this dance, Lily?'

I was so surprised that at first I could only stare at him. But his expression held an invitation I couldn't refuse, a look so gentle and warm that of course I said, 'Thank you, Mr Daniel. I should love to dance with you.'

He nodded and led me into the middle of the room which, I saw, had been cleared to make a space. Then he held out his arms, saying — almost whispering, 'I have been waiting for this moment since the first time you came into my life, sweet Lily.'

Then the music washed over me, the gentle strains and rhythm helping me to follow his lead as we slowly danced in the middle of the room. He held me very close, the warmth and strength of his body releasing all my senses. I allowed my head to rest on his shoulder, his face only inches away, and it was the most wonderful moment in

my whole life. I felt I had found the place where I should be, and wanted to remain there always. Yes, I loved Daniel, and I was happy.

When the music ended we stopped. I looked into his face and realised he looked as happy as I felt. My voice was unsteady as I said, 'You have to wind it up again, I think, Mr Daniel.'

At once he shook his head and said rapidly, 'Never use that title again, sweet Lily. It's Daniel from now on — except, of course, when you wish to talk about us formally, and then it will be Mr and Mrs Daniel Frobisher.'

I gasped, hardly believing what he said. 'Mr and Mrs . . . ?' No words came, but he was laughing, holding me close to him, his voice full of warmth and love as he said quickly, 'Yes, sweet Lily, because of course I'm asking you to marry me. What do you say?'

I could say nothing. But I knew that actions would be more expressive than mere words, so I looked up into his eyes, threw my arms around his neck,

drew his head down and kissed him. Never before had I known such pleasure. We kissed for a long time until our breath ran out, and then he grabbed me and kissed me again, only letting me free for a second, to ask, 'Well? Your answer please, Lily, and at once!'

Laughter took the place of words for a moment, until at last I was able to splutter, 'Yes! Yes, and yes, Daniel! Of course I'll marry you. And now, please kiss me again!'

17

I shall never forget that evening. The excitement of telling Mrs Hodge when she came in with the coffee, with Nancy standing outside the door listening, and everyone smiling, smiling! Daniel wound up the gramophone and put on a different record, and we danced again together, our bodies warm and close. Bedtime came at last and he escorted me upstairs to my room beside the nursery, leaving me at the door, kissing me again and whispering, 'Not long before we have our own bedroom, my darling Lily. But until then, sleep well, with sweet dreams.'

I had no dreams, and awoke with a memory of all that had happened filling my head as I lay in bed, with the morning sun shafting through the window and filling me with happiness. I

put on my wrapper and went next door to awaken Mary and help her wash and dress, thinking about telling her that I was to be her new mama, and would she be pleased or not, when I opened the bedroom door and saw — an empty bed.

I stared at it. Then I saw her walking shoes were gone, also her coat and hat. It took me only a few minutes to dress myself and rush downstairs into the dining room where I found Daniel, greeting me with a wonderful smile. I gave him no time to speak but simply said rapidly, 'Mary has disappeared, Daniel. She's gone out. We must go and find her.'

His frown was terrible, and I knew how he felt. I pulled on a shawl and secured my hat, and together we went into the hall, only pausing to call Mrs Hodge and tell her where we were going.

She came out of the kitchen looking pale and worried. 'Gone, has she? Oh, the little mite. But wherever she's gone

she's taken a big slice of your chocolate cake, Miss Lily! I found the tin open and a wedge cut out! I thought she might have taken it for her breakfast, but — oh dear, oh dear!'

I tried to reassure her. 'We'll soon find her, Mrs Hodge. Try not to worry.'

I followed Daniel out into the garden, pausing at the gate to make plans. He said, 'I'll go along the seafront — maybe she's gone to the pier. You go the other way.'

'To the café, and then the bakery. She can't have gone far. Oh, Daniel . . . '

He took my hands and pressed them, saying, 'Don't look like that, my darling. We'll soon have her home.'

I nodded, tried to check the sobs heaving in my chest, and turned, running down the street, heading for Jess and the café. Jess looked up, surprised, when I burst in. 'Goodness, you're out early, Lily. But — something the matter?'

I could hardly speak for the fear filling me, but unsteadily I managed a

few words. 'Yes, Mary has disappeared. Have you seen her, Jess?'

'No. But perhaps Bobby might know; he's just come back with the bread.' She went to the back room and called, 'Bobby, have you seen Miss Mary?'

He came out into the café, chewing on a crust of new bread. 'I saw her going down the road, towards the river beach. She smiled when I passed her, and ran on.'

My heart leaped. 'The river beach? The boats, the water — oh no!' I was out and running before Jess could reply. Only a few seconds and I was there, sand kicking up all over my boots and the sun glinting on the fast-flowing river. I could hardly see, but walked steadily down the beach towards the Point, all the time scanning the water. A small child in a straw hat with flowers decorating it, and a check coat . . . *Please don't let her be there.*

And then a familiar voice. Matt appeared out of his boat house and called. 'Lily! She's here, all safe, but wet

through. Come up here.'

I turned away from the river, and there he was, coming towards me, smiling over his shoulder at someone I couldn't see. I ran to him. 'Mary? Where is she?'

He took my hand and led me into the shadowy boathouse. There she was, sitting in his old chair — safe, alive and smiling. I breathed a prayer of thankfulness and went to her side. Her hands were wet and covered with something sticky and dark and then, out of all the fear and despair, a familiar smell returned me slowly to normal. Chocolate.

Kneeling beside her, I put my arms around her wet little body and kissed the upturned face with its hesitant smile. 'How did you get so wet, Mary?' I asked.

She wriggled, looking ashamed and not nearly as happy as she usually was. 'I knew Becky wanted a piece of your cake, Lily,' she whispered at last, hiding her face for a moment, 'and so I

brought her one. I thought she was probably on the boat, 'cause you said she lived there, and so I climbed on. When I saw Matt climbing on, too, I hid behind a big old oilskin. I thought he'd be angry. But I couldn't see Becky anywhere. Then, as the boat moved, I lost my balance and fell into the water. Oh, it was cold! The chocolate cake went in, too.' She looked at me again, and now the sky-blue eyes were smiling. 'Are you angry with me, Lily? And what will Papa say? Oh dear, I've been a bad girl, I know . . . but I was only trying to share your lovely cake with Becky, you see.'

There was a shadow in the doorway of the boathouse, and we both looked up to see Daniel entering. He exchanged glances with me — relief, warmth, love — and then bent over Mary, who threw her arms around his neck. I could just hear her whisper in his ear, 'I'm sorry, Papa. I'll never be naughty again. I don't like boats and the water anymore — it's so wet and cold, and I want to go home

and grow flowers instead. Can I do that, please?'

Daniel muffled his laughter and hugged her very tightly. He looked at me and we both smiled. I said apologetically, 'Of course this is all my fault, telling Mary stories about Becky. I'm sorry, too, Daniel. Can you forgive us both?'

He stood up, one hand still holding Mary's, and said to me very quietly, 'My darling Lily, I would forgive you anything — and this is nothing to be blamed for. I feel pretty sure that Mary won't have much time for Becky in the future — not after this wet and rather frightening little adventure. We'll see, won't we? But now to get her home and dry.'

Matt turned to me and then looked at Daniel, saying, 'Will you let me carry the little maid down to Regent Row, to Miss Lily's aunt's bakery, sir? Her big oven will be the driest place, you see, and you and Miss Lily can follow us there.'

Relief rushed through me. So Matt had accepted that Daniel and I needed to be together, and clearly he would no longer be waiting for me to return to him. I smiled and saw how his tanned face eased out into an answering smile. I said gratefully, 'That would be wonderful. Thank you, Matt.'

Daniel said wryly, 'It's good of you, but you'll get very damp, I'm afraid, even if you wrap her in a blanket.'

Matt grinned as he reached out to find a blanket lying near Mary's chair. 'Better me in old clothes than you in your good jacket, sir.'

I saw them exchange amused glances as he wrapped up Mary and then caught her in his arms. 'You're a good man,' Daniel said gratefully.

We waited until Matt and his burden were out of the boathouse, he striding along the beach and disappearing down the road leading to the bakery. We followed them, Daniel's arm supporting mine as we made our way through thick sand and the

Other titles in the
Linford Romance Library:

GRACIE'S WAR

Elaine Everest

Britain is at war — but young Gracie Sayers and her best friend Peggy are determined they will still have fun, enjoying cinema trips and dances with Peggy's young man Colin and her cousin Joe. However, there is something shifty about Joe, and Gracie finds she much prefers Colin's friend, the kind and decent Tony. Then, one night, a terrible event changes everything. Now Tony is away at war — and Gracie is carrying the wrong man's child . . .

CUPCAKES AND CANDLESTICKS

Nora Fountain

When Maddy's husband Rob suddenly announces that he's leaving her and moving to Canada with his pretty young employee, her world comes crashing down. As Rob's promises of financial support prove worthless, Maddy finds herself under growing pressure to forge a new life for herself and her four children. She decides to start a catering business, but will it earn enough money — and is that what she really wants? And then she meets the gorgeous Guy in the strangest of circumstances . . .

FLIGHT OF THE HERON

Susan Udy

On her deathbed, Christie's mother confides to her daughter that she has family she never knew existed — grandparents, a great-aunt, and an uncle — and elicits a promise from Christie to travel to Devon to meet them. When she arrives, she's surprised to find another man living there: the leonine and captivating Lucas Grant. But when her grandmother decides to change her will and leave Christie a sizeable inheritance, it's soon all too evident that someone wants to get rid of her, and both her uncle and Lucas have a motive . . .

seaweed-encrusted tideline. I looked at the river, grey-green and fast-flowing, impersonal, beautiful yet dangerous, and in my heart I thanked fate — and Matt — for bringing little Mary safely back to us.

The bakery was warm and bustling with life when we reached it. Mary sat in Aunt Edie's old armchair right beside the huge oven, her face already pink and glowing, her clothes gently steaming, while my mother knelt at her side, holding her hands, listening to the story Mary was enthusiastically telling her. 'And so, you see, I don't think I want to know any more about Becky, because — did you know?' Her voice rose and Mother's eyebrows raised. 'I shall be going to school soon, and then I shall make real friends. That'll be after we've moved into the big house . . . And yes, I shall be able to play in your little cottage, Mrs Drew! Will you come and tell me how to grow your lovely flowers?'

I turned closer to Daniel and

murmured, 'We don't have to say a word, do we? Mary's told them everything!'

Daniel laughed and put his arms around me. 'But they don't know that we're going to be married, do they, sweetheart? Hold your breath; I'll tell them.'

I found one of the old stools I used to rest on and sat down. What would Mother say? What would Aunt Edie think? And Mary — would she be pleased at the amazing news?

I had no reason to worry once Daniel had said the magic words: 'Lily has said she will be my wife — your new mama, Mary. And you, Mrs Drew, are to be our new tenant in the little cottage where you grow your flowers, and as Mary has already decreed, where you can teach her to be a gardener rather than a very wet water baby!'

I sat there on the uncomfortable stool while congratulations and loving kisses were showered on me. Even Daniel came in for a hug from my mother, who then coloured and almost begged his pardon. But how we laughed; how happy we all felt as warmth and love filled the untidy, flour-dusty bakery. The smell of new bread scented the air and Aunt Edie, smiling determinedly, declared we must have a cup of tea and some hot crusty bread to honour the occasion.

'Always knew the maid would have a good life, once she got used to hard work,' she said, and then we laughed some more.

* * *

Much later, in the quietness of the big house on the Esplanade, we watched Mary — dry, freshly clothed and happy — as she left the luncheon table and headed upstairs, saying, 'I'm going to find my book about flowers. I shall have to know a lot about them, if we're going to grow a garden No, don't come, Lily. I'm quite cap — capable of doing things on my own now I'm a big girl, you know.'

Daniel and I looked at each other as we heard her race up the stairs. Then he drew out my chair, held me very close, and whispered, 'We're together, my love. Is it enough?'

I put my arms around his neck and whispered back, safe in the warmth of his strong embrace, 'It's all I ever wanted, Daniel. You and I; and Mary, growing up.'

My heart was beating fast as I realised that the love it held was being shared. And returned. Oh yes, all I'd ever dreamed of.

THE END